Richard and ~~[barcode]~~ Chris back to their c~~[barcode]~~ed. He gripped Susan's arm tightly. "Wait a second. What was that?"

"I didn't hear anything." Nervously, Susan looked around. "What did it sound like?"

"I'm not sure. . . . Maybe it was nothing. It's just that all of a sudden, I had this creepy feeling that we were being followed."

They stood still for a full minute—but heard nothing. It was Chris who finally broke the silence. "Listen, I think that instead of running away, we should go after whoever's following us."

"Okay," said Alan. "If that's how everybody feels, why don't we break up into couples and take a quick look around?"

Then the four of them heard a loud noise that made them all jump.

"Somebody just slammed a car door," said Alan.

"Let's follow him!" cried Chris. "Quick, where's the pickup?"

STRAWBERRY
SUMMER

Cynthia Blair

FAWCETT JUNIPER • NEW YORK

RLI: $\dfrac{\text{VL: 5 \& up}}{\text{IL: 6 \& up}}$

A Fawcett Juniper Book
Published by Ballantine Books

Library of Congress Catalog Card Number: 86-90885

ISBN: 0-449-70183-2

Manufactured in the United States of America

First Edition: July 1986
Fourth Printing: June 1988

One

"Attention, passengers. The bus for Lake Majestic is now boarding. Now calling all passengers for Lake Majestic!"

As the announcement came over the loudspeaker of the Whittington bus station, two travelers who'd just been dropped off at the side door began to scurry.

"That's our bus, Chris!" cried Susan Pratt as the girls hurried across the bus station toward the departure area. "We'd better hurry!"

"Oh, I'm sure we have plenty of time. That was probably just the first call." But Christine Pratt, Susan's twin sister, broke into a slow run.

It was no easy matter, trying to rush with a heavy suitcase in one hand and the huge bag lunch their mother had packed for them in the other. Chris suddenly found herself wondering what would happen if her suitcase burst open, as she feared it might, right there in the middle of the Whittington bus station. The whole summer's clothes would spill out onto the floor: shorts, T-shirts, bathing suits, sundresses, sandals, and sneakers. Not wanting to leave anything behind, she had packed everything she could possibly think of. Everything, as her mother had joked, except her winter coat.

Susan, on the other hand, had packed much more sensibly. Just two or three of everthing—one to wash, one to wear, one extra, just in case. The suitcase she carried was much smaller and much lighter. She'd even had enough room to pack a few paperback novels she hoped to read in the next few weeks, during whatever moments of leisure she managed to grab, as well as a pad of drawing paper and a box of her favorite pastels.

If Susan's suitcase ever opened up by accident, Chris thought, smiling to herself, everyone in the bus station would probably be awestruck by how well-organized my twin sister is!

"Here, let me carry our lunch," Susan offered, noticing the difficulty her twin was having. "I can manage that besides my suitcase."

"We probably should have eaten it in the car on the way over here. Then we wouldn't have to carry it at all!"

Chris's suggestion made the two of them burst out laughing.

"Don't worry, dear twin," Susan said when she'd caught her breath. "We've got plenty of time. It's just that I'm so excited that I can't wait to be on that bus, on our way to Lake Majestic!"

While the two sixteen-year-olds were identical twins, Susan and Chris looked hardly alike at all as they stashed their suitcases in the bus's storage compartment down below and scrambled aboard. They both had the same dark brown eyes, shoulder-length chestnut hair, and facial features: high cheekbones, ski-jump noses, and winning smiles. But today, like most of the time, their similarities were hardly noticeable, masked as they were by their more obvious differences in appearance, definitely reflections of the differences in their personalities.

Chris, the more outgoing of the two, liked to dress fashionably. She was wearing a pair of pink jeans with a bright pink, blue, and green blouse that was one of her favorites. The blue barrettes in her hair, her oversize pink earrings, and the other gaily colored jewelry she wore all seemed to complement her cheerful, talkative personality.

Susan, meanwhile, preferred a good book or a few hours at an easel, painting landscapes or portraits or just about anything. And she tended to dress with much less flamboyance than her twin. Today, for example, she had donned a white blouse and a simple flowered skirt for the long bus trip ahead. Her hair was pulled back into a ponytail, designed to minimize the effects of the July heat. And the only jewelry she wore was a pair of simple earrings, the tiny hoops made of delicate gold that her parents had given her for her sixteenth birthday.

Once they had found seats on the bus and were finally settled in, both girls sighed with relief.

"We made it!" Susan nestled their big lunch bag between them. "And now that we've got a three-hour ride ahead of us, I'm really glad we didn't eat all this food already!"

"I'm so excited, Sooz!" Chris was staring out the window at the other people who were lining up to get on the bus. "The two of us getting jobs as camp counselors for the summer was one of the best ideas you've ever had!"

"Thanks, but it wasn't exactly my idea, remember? It was Mom's."

"Oh, that's right. Once she saw how bored we were getting, she realized she'd better come up with *something* for us to do!"

Chris laughed as she thought about how the summer had started, with her lying in the hammock in the backyard, complaining about the fact that she had absolutely no plans for the next two months. Applying for camp counselor positions at Camp Pinewood and half a dozen other camps nearby had been their mother's solution.

It wasn't until they both were accepted for a six-week stint, from mid-July until the end of August, that Chris and Susan realized how much they'd been hoping it would work out. It was late to be applying, they knew, and they were pleased and surprised at being hired. Susan was going to be a counselor in arts and crafts, her favorite hobby as well as the area in which she was most talented. She even hoped to go on to art school after graduating from high school. Chris was going to teach swimming, something that her lifelong interest in the sport prepared her for well.

Beyond their special interests in art and swimming, the Pratt twins were simply looking forward to spending the summer out of doors. Being camp counselors, they reasoned, had to be almost as much fun as being a kid at a summer camp. According to the brochures they'd received along with the acceptance letters, Camp Pinewood offered boating, hiking, archery, and nature walks. And making some new friends was something else they wouldn't have the chance to do if they stayed at home in Whittington. All in all, it seemed as if their mother had come up with the perfect way to spend their seventeenth summer.

"Well, I just hope they don't work us too hard," Chris complained cheerfully, leaning back comfortably in her seat as the bus driver slammed the door closed and started up the engine. "Over the next six weeks, I intend to indulge in every single one of my favorite summertime pleasures."

"We know for sure you'll have a chance to do some swimming," Susan teased. "And I'll certainly have time to work on some new art projects."

"I'm talking about all those things that make summer the very best season of the year. Like getting a gorgeous tan . . ."

"And drinking lemonade."

"Catching fireflies—and then letting them go."

"Going barefoot. Don't forget that!" Susan couldn't help wiggling her toes at the mere thought.

"And what about eating strawberries?" Chris closed her eyes and smiled dreamily. "Ummm, I *love* strawberries. I hope Camp Pinewood has them for dessert every night at dinner. Strawberry shortcake, strawberries and cream, strawberries on vanilla ice cream . . ."

"It's true; it just doesn't feel like summer without strawberries," Susan agreed. "Well, no matter what happens, one thing's for sure."

"What?"

"This is definitely an adventure!"

"Not exactly our usual kind of adventure, either!" Chris's brown eyes were twinkling as she turned to face her sister.

Susan knew exactly what her twin was talking about. Twice before, the Pratt girls had created their own "adventures" by trading identities, pretending to be each other. The first time, they had bet on whether or not they could switch places—Chris becoming Susan, Susan becoming Chris—for a full two weeks without having anyone figure out what was going on. The purpose had been for each girl to find out what the other's life was like. The stakes of the bet had been a banana split. That little caper, which they had nicknamed the Banana Split Affair, had convinced them that they really could pull off a scheme like that—and learn a lot while doing it.

The second time had been earlier that summer. When Chris had been selected as the honorary "Queen" in their hometown's celebration of its hundredth anniversary, she and Susan took turns at being Christine Pratt. It seemed only fair, since Chris had been chosen on the basis of a history project that in reality both girls had worked on together. And while they had been slightly less successful in this second attempt of theirs, it had all ended up working out fine. The celebration at the end of the Hot Fudge Sunday Affair, as they dubbed that week of trading identities, was well deserved.

"I think that for the rest of the summer, we'd better hang on to our own identities," Susan said with a rueful grin. "I don't know about you, but I find it much easier to be *me* than anybody else— even my very own twin."

"Then I guess I'll just have to be content with being Chris Pratt for a while. Unless, of course, something comes up . . ."

"Oh, no!" Susan groaned, pretending to be

exasperated. "Enough! I want to live my life as *Susan* for a change!"

"Well, okay . . . I guess. But let's keep in mind that switching places is always a possibility. After all, what good is having a twin sister if you can't pretend to *be* her every now and then?"

"All right. We'll see."

Despite her protests, Susan knew that her twin was fully aware that she had enjoyed those two escapades as much as Chris.

Susan let her thoughts drift to Camp Pinewood. Neither of the girls had ever been there. They knew little about it, aside from what they'd seen in the few pictures in the brochures they'd received in the mail. Yet here she was, traveling there on a bus, prepared to spend six whole weeks at this place she'd never even seen. For the first time, she began to feel butterflies in her stomach. This really *was* a kind of adventure. . . .

"Hey, Sooz?" Chris interrupted her daydreaming. She sounded unusually serious.

"Yes?"

"I wonder what Camp Pinewood is going to be like." It was as if her sister had read her mind—not the first time one twin had a kind of sixth sense about what the other was thinking or feeling. "I wonder if it's big or little, modern or old-fashioned. . . ."

"Well, no matter what it turns out to look like, you and I have already got one advantage over all the other counselors going to work there for the summer."

"What's that?" Chris was genuinely puzzled.

"We're both bringing along a built-in friend!"

Both girls found that thought extremely comforting. The spell of nervousness that had plagued them momentarily vanished as quickly as it arrived.

Chris glanced at her watch. "Gee, we've already been on the road a good fifteen minutes."

"So?"

"So, I don't know about you, but I'm getting hungry."

"But Chris! It's eleven o'clock in the morning!"

"I know. But aren't you dying to know what's in this tremendous lunch Mom packed for us?"

The two girls exchanged mischievous glances, then pounced upon the big brown paper bag sitting between them.

"Here's some juice, and napkins, and straws. . . . And these look like tuna fish sandwiches." Susan arranged everything she had retrieved from the bag in her lap while Chris delved in further.

"Oh, yum! Look, Sooz, some of Mom's home-made peanut butter cookies."

"And what's this, in this container?" Puzzled, Susan pried the cover off a small round plastic jar.

"Oh, look!" Chris exclaimed. She put aside the rest of the lunch goodies, no longer interested in any of them. "Strawberries!"

Chris and Susan looked at each other and burst out laughing. Suddenly, the two girls realized what high hopes they had for the rest of their summer. And they both had the feeling it was going to live up to every one of their expectations.

TWO

"*What do you think, Sooz?*" gulped Chris. "*Do you think we're in the wrong place?*"

The taxi the twins had hailed at the bus station had just dropped them off at the side of the road, the driver insisting that this was where they wanted to be. And sure enough, in front of the driveway where they now stood there was a wooden sign reading "Camp Pinewood." But the sign was split and badly in need of repainting, the driveway was overgrown with weeds at the edges, and there seemed to be no one else around for miles. The two girls stood at the side of the road, clutching their suitcases nervously, not quite sure of exactly what to do next.

"Well, there's only one way to find out," Susan said bravely. "This driveway must lead some-where. Let's follow it and see what Camp Pinewood is all about." Feeling very much like Dorothy in *The Wizard of Oz,* she started down the road.

Chris, still hanging back hesitantly, finally gave in and followed her.

"You don't suppose this place is *haunted,* do you?"

"You've seen too many movies, Chris! Besides, I think I see signs of civilization. Look, there's a house up ahead!"

"And look! There's the lake! Oh, Sooz, it's gorgeous!" Chris, awestruck, dropped her suitcase in the road and ran to the edge, where she could get a better look. "I had no idea it would be so huge!"

It was true; Lake Majestic, seen from atop the hill they were on, was truly impressive. It was tremendous, much larger than Chris had ever imagined. Its crystal-clear blue surface was illuminated by bursts of sunlight, caught on the gentle waves created by light breezes. Far in the distance, small groups of buildings dotted the shoreline.

Other camps, Chris surmised. Which led her right back to their original dilemma: where was Camp Pinewood?

"We're in the right place, all right. A lake that size and that beautiful just *has* to be called Lake Majestic. Now all we need to do is find Camp Pinewood."

Feeling encouraged, the girls trudged on a bit further down the driveway, suitcases in hand. By this point, even Susan's was starting to feel heavy. Neither bothered to try making conversation. So when the sound of the engine of a distant car or truck buzzed through the air, they both perked up right away.

"Here comes somebody," Susan said hopefully.

"I just hope it's not a ghost," Chris muttered. "Or a car that's driving itself!"

She was almost relieved to see that it wasn't.

Instead, it was a battered-up old pickup truck—exactly the kind of vehicle she would have expected to see on a desolate road like this one. It came chugging toward them, sounding as if it might not make it to wherever it was going. When it slowed down near them, both Chris and Susan were surprised to see that its driver was a boy about their age, with straight black hair, green eyes, and a rather sullen expression.

"Can I help you girls?" he asked, leaning out the window and eyeing them warily.

"What does he think we are, cat burglars?" Chris muttered, angered by his tone.

But Susan was more forgiving—and more practical. "I'm Susan Pratt, and this is my sister, Christine. We're looking for Camp Pinewood. Are we in the right place?"

"Yeah, you're in the right place."

"Oh, good! We're camp counselors. Chris's speciality is swimming, and I'm teaching arts and crafts. . . ."

"Yeah, I know all about you."

Chris and Susan exchanged glances. He was certainly one of the surlier people they'd encountered lately. That same feeling that had hit them when they'd climbed out of the taxi, that feeling of "What have we done *now*?" swept over them once again.

"Well, then," said Chris, "maybe you could give us a lift to the camp." She couldn't resist adding, "These suitcases aren't exactly light, you know."

The boy just grunted. But he leaned over and opened the door of the pickup, signifying that they should get in.

Once they were on their way, their heavy suitcases in back and the scattered buildings of Camp Pinewood just starting to come into view, Susan started to perk up once again.

"So, do you work here, too?"

"Sort of," the boy mumbled. "My parents run Camp Pinewood. They're the owners. So I always spend my summers helping out around the place."

"That sounds like fun."

The boy just grunted. They drove the rest of the way in silence.

As they rode further along, deeper into the woods and closer to Lake Majestic, Camp Pinewood gradually emerged around them. Groups of cabins built from logs were nestled among the trees, along the side of the road. Then a small infirmary, a large flat building that looked like a dining hall, and a few other buildings of various sizes, all of them with the same rustic flavor of the cabins. Susan surmised that one of them must be the arts and crafts building, where she would be spending a lot of her time. She also caught a glimpse of what looked like a boathouse, down by the shore of Lake Majestic.

Camp Pinewood was beginning to show some promise. But she was still surprised by how run-down it looked. There was something almost sad about the place.

It's just because the kids haven't arrived yet, she told herself. Once they get here, I'm sure this will turn into a lively camp where everybody has lots of fun. Including Chris and me!

But the somber look on Chris's face told her that her twin's initial reaction to the camp was the same as hers.

The boy pulled up in front of a house, the first building the girls had spotted from up on the driveway. It was a friendly place, with white shingles, blue shutters, and a sagging front porch, perched on top of a small hill so that it looked out over the camp.

"This is where my folks live," he said. "Come on, and I'll introduce you."

Fortunately, Jake and Olive Reed were a lot friendlier than their son. They rushed out to greet their two new counselors as soon as they heard the sputtering engine of the pickup in front of their house.

"Welcome to Camp Pinewood!" Olive Reed, a heavyset woman with her son's coloring and features, hurried over, wearing a big smile. "Either I'm seeing double or you two are the Pratt twins, Christine and Susan. I'm pleased to meet you. Come on in and have some iced tea. Alan, dear, the girls will be staying in Cabin Four. Would you mind dropping their suitcases there when you have a chance?"

It was only then that the girls found out what the Reeds' son's name was. He certainly hadn't volunteered that information, and asking him right out would have somehow seemed too much like prying.

"Now, which one of you is Chris, and which is Susan?" Mrs. Reed asked once she had sat down with them and her husband at the kitchen table, where they all had a glass of iced tea. Alan had declined to join them, saying he had too much to do, what with the opening of camp the very next day and all.

"Even more important," said Mr. Reed with a chuckle, "how can we tell you two apart?" Like his wife, he was squarely built, with dark hair, a tanned, lined face, and large, strong hands.

The twins laughed. "Actually, we're very different," Chris explained. "Not only our personalities, but also the way we dress and wear our hair . . ."

"Chris is right. We're very easy to tell apart—unless we *want* to look the same, of course." She cast a teasing glance in her twin's direction. "As a matter of fact, we happen to be experts in the field of fooling people. We've got quite a bit of experience in that area.

"But don't worry," she hastened to add, anxious to put her new employers at ease. "We're not about to trick anybody this summer. Right, Chris?" She gave her sister a meaningful look.

As they drank their iced tea, the Reeds told them about the camp and filled them in on the details of their duties as camp counselors. The campers, aged eight to twelve, were due to arrive at camp the next day, a day that promised to be busy if not chaotic. Some of the other counselors had already arrived; the rest would be coming in first thing in the morning. The average day's schedule was a full one, but there was time for relaxing—and even doing some swimming or boating on one's own.

"How many campers are coming tomorrow?" Susan asked, wondering, once again, if perhaps she was getting in over her head.

The look that Jake and Olive Reed exchanged told her that she had touched a soft spot.

"A lot fewer than last year," Mr. Reed said, suddenly somber. "And that was fewer than the year before. . . ."

"Yes, it's true," his wife admitted. "Business has been falling off lately. But we're still managing."

"Just barely." Mr. Reed stood up. "Listen, I'd better not get started on this. Alan's right; there's still a lot that has to get done before tomorrow. It's an important day for us, and we've got to be ready."

When he had gone, letting the kitchen's screen door slam behind him, Mrs. Reed looked at the twins sadly. "I don't think this is the kind of thing we should be worrying our counselors with, but Jake has good reason to be disturbed. Alan's very upset, too. The truth is, there have been some peculiar things going on around here the last couple of years. And they're both afraid that it's going to start up again this summer, once the season gets rolling."

"What exactly has been going on?" Susan asked softly.

"Well, it's hard to describe." Mrs. Reed toyed with her iced tea glass nervously. "Just a lot of strange things. Supplies disappearing, then turning up in some unlikely place. Dishes getting broken.

One morning—the morning of Parents' Day, in fact—we all woke up to find someone had cut all our boats loose. Sailboats, canoes, rowboats—even the rafts and the life preservers. It wasn't serious, of course. We did manage to get them all back, after spending hours going around the lake, retrieving them. But it was pretty embarrassing when all the parents showed up, wanting to see what their children had learned about boating over the summer.''

"Surely the parents understood that it wasn't your fault!" Chris interjected.

Mrs. Reed shook her head slowly. "We've been losing a lot of business. With all the confusion, a lot of the kids just don't come back the following summer. Their parents find them other camps to go to. Some of them even right here on Lake Majestic." Her eyes had become glazed with tears. "The way things are going, it looks as if Mr. Reed and I may have to close the camp before too long. As it is, the camp itself is already beginning to suffer. You can see for yourselves how run-down things are getting. We just don't have the money to maintain it properly."

All three of them were silent for a while, pretending to be intent on finishing up their iced tea. Mrs. Reed dabbed at her eyes with the edge of her napkin.

"Well, enough about all that. This is supposed to be a happy occasion. After all, it's your first day at Camp Pinewood! Goodness, what are you two going to think, with me going on and on like this?

"Now, why don't you both scoot on up to Cabin Four and get settled in? Just follow the path, right outside. The buildings are well marked. Dinner's at six, in the big dining hall. We always ring a bell at dinnertime; if you get lost, just follow the clanging. And I really do want to welcome you to Camp Pinewood. I'm sure you'll both have a wonderful summer!"

But as Chris and Susan made their way up the hill, toward the cabins, the somber mood followed them.

"That sure was a strange story Mrs. Reed told us," said Chris.

"I'll say. Strange—and very upsetting."

"Sounds almost like ghosts are up to something."

"Sounds more like troublemakers to me!" Susan declared angrily. "The *human* variety! Imagine someone sabotaging Camp Pinewood like that! And imagine someone wanting to hurt Mr. and Mrs. Reed! They're such sweet people, both of them. And they're just trying to run a nice camp for children. Make a living for themselves."

"It is mysterious." Chris dug her hands into the pockets of her pink jeans. "I wish there was something we could do to help."

"Maybe there is. But first we have to find out more about what's going on around here."

"Right. But even before that, we have to turn this place into a home away from home!"

The girls had just reached Cabin Four. It was a tiny, simple building, almost like a wooden tent. An elevated wooden platform, a sloped roof, and walls that were only waist-high. The only furniture was four cots. At the foot of each was an old-fashioned trunk.

"Plenty of fresh air," Chris muttered. "I just hope the raccoons don't get us."

"I'd rather fight off raccoons than mosquitoes!" Susan plopped onto the bed. Its springs creaked loudly under her weight. "Not exactly the Holiday Inn, is it?"

"It looks like we'll have company, too. Two more roommates . . . other counselors, I guess." Chris, too, sank onto one of the cots. "You know what, Sooz?"

"What?"

"I suddenly have a terrible feeling that this is going to turn out to be a long summer. Maybe even a long, *long* summer!"

For once in her life, Susan couldn't think of anything optimistic to say.

Three

The three-hour bus trip, the excitement and confu-
sion of being in a new place, and initial apprehen-
sions about Camp Pinewood had taken their toll.
Chris and Susan slept late the next morning, their
sleep made even deeper than usual by all the fresh
air. Even the bright morning sunlight streaming
through the open walls of their cabin failed to rouse
them.

It wasn't until two girls came into Cabin Four,
talking and laughing and banging their suitcases
against the metal frames of the beds, that the twins
woke up.

"Who's there?" Chris, still groggy, demanded as
she sat up in bed.

Susan, lying in the cot beside her, opened her
eyes wide. She was awake instantly.

"Oh, sorry! We didn't realize anybody was in
here." One of the girls who had just come in

dropped her suitcase onto one of the trunks. She had curly blond hair, round blue eyes, and lots of freckles.

"What time is it?" Susan was already bounding out of bed.

"Just past nine." The other girl, tall and thin with long red hair, glanced around the cabin, then claimed as her own the only bed that was left. She looked at Chris and Susan more carefully. "Hey, are you two sisters?"

Chris, finally awake, was climbing out of bed. "We're twins. I'm Chris Pratt, and this is Susan."

"Pleased to meet you! I've never known a pair of twins before." The redheaded girl grinned. "It'll be an honor to share Cabin Four with you. My name is Linda Ames."

"And I'm Samantha Collier. But everybody calls me Sam," the other girl piped up. "And I've never known any twins either!"

Susan laughed. "We're not any different from anybody else."

"Right," Chris agreed. "My sister and I just happen to share the same face, that's all!"

While Chris and Susan slipped into shorts and T-shirts, Sam and Linda unpacked.

"Is this your first camp counseling job?" asked Linda. Along with her clothes, Susan noticed that she unpacked a pile of paperback novels—including a few that she had been anxious to read herself.

"Yes. In fact, Chris and I never even heard of Camp Pinewood until a few weeks ago. How about you?"

"This is the third summer here for both Sam and

me. But," she added with a sad smile, "I have a feeling it might turn out to be our last."

Chris and Susan exchanged knowing looks. So their two cabinmates were also aware of the mysterious things that had been going on at the camp! Before they could ask about how much they knew, Linda volunteered the information.

"Yes, Camp Pinewood has been running into some financial difficulties, all because of some strange goings-on that no one's been able to figure out. The number of kids who come here each summer keeps getting smaller, year after year." She sighed. "As much as I'd hate to see it, it looks like Mr. and Mrs. Reed might even have to close down after this season."

The four girls were quiet for a few moments as they thought about the terrible fate that seemed destined to befall the Reed family, for reasons that were entirely out of their control.

"Well," Linda finally said, "there's no use in us worrying about that right now. What we can do is make sure that all the kids who *do* come to Camp Pinewood have a great summer! They should start arriving in a couple of hours. In the meantime, anyone for breakfast?"

"I'm ready for a *second* breakfast." Sam grinned. "I've been on a bus since seven, and even though I ate when I woke up, it seems so long ago that I can't even remember what I ate!"

"The cook always makes sure there's lots of food around on the first day of camp," Linda explained. "I'll bet if we go down to the dining hall, there'll be an entire feast waiting for us. Eggs, sausages, cereal—anything you want!"

"I sure hope so," said Chris. "I'm starving!"

The four girls trooped off in search of breakfast. Already it was obvious to Chris and Susan that they and their new cabinmates were going to become fast friends.

After a breakfast that was just as hearty as Linda had promised it would be, Chris went down to the lake, anxious to check out the boathouse and see if she could find any of the other counselors who taught swimming. Susan ventured off in search of the arts and crafts building. With the campers arriving soon, she wanted to get an idea of what kinds of supplies she had to work with.

The arts and crafts building was like an old-fashioned schoolhouse. It consisted of a single room, with lots of light and air streaming in through the huge windows that were on all four sides. The furniture was simple: big tables, chairs, and shelves, everything made of wood. She felt at home there immediately.

All it needs, she thought, is some color. And as soon as I get the kids involved with paints and crayons, every square inch of the walls will be covered with their artwork!

Then she noticed a small door at the back of the room. Wanting to become familiar with every aspect of her new "classroom," she walked over to see where it led. It was not until she got close that she noticed it was slightly ajar. Even though it was dark inside, she surmised that it was a closet of some sort—probably a storage closet for supplies. But as she reached for the knob, planning to pull the door open, she jumped.

Something was moving inside! She was certain she heard someone . . . or something.

Susan's heart began to pound. She suddenly realized that she was all alone. Everyone else was down by the lake or back at the cabins. Yet she was unable to move. She just stood there, her eyes glued to the blackness beyond the opened door, listening.

And then, with a loud creak, the door began to swing open slowly. Susan could scarcely breathe.

Run! Run! she thought wildly. But she didn't. She stayed perfectly still, watching and waiting, as if paralyzed.

The door opened wider, the blackness of the closet faded as the room's light seeped in—and a boy emerged, his sandy hair covered with dust and his expression apologetic.

Susan gasped, partly from surprise, but even more from relief.

"What on earth are you *doing* in there?" she cried.

"I hope I didn't startle you. . . . Did I?"

"Oh, no. Not at all. I was just . . . surprised, that's all."

The boy laughed. "Well, you're as white as a ghost. By the way, that's not by any chance what you thought *I* was, was it?"

"No, of course not!" At first, Susan tried to sound indignant. But then she started to laugh, too. "But I certainly wasn't expecting a living creature to emerge from the storage closet!" She peered inside. "That *is* what this is, isn't it? A storage closet, for art supplies?"

"Yes. And, I'm pleased to report, it seems that everything's there, for a change. At least, from what I could tell before the light bulb burned out and left me standing in the dark." He looked down at his dust-covered shirt and hands. "I guess I *do* look sort of like a ghost, don't I!"

Susan's brown eyes narrowed with curiosity. "What exactly did you mean when you said 'everything's there, for a change'?"

"Oh, nothing, really. It's just that I was here last year, too, as an arts and crafts counselor. And we had some, um, problems with things disappearing. Boxes of crayons, paper . . . things like that. Never anything very valuable. But the funny thing was, they'd always turn up a few days later. In the last place you'd ever expect, too. Like the dining hall, or even out in the woods. Frankly, it was more of an annoyance than anything else. And it always seemed to happen at the most inconvenient times. I'd promise the kids that the next day they could finally work with clay, and they'd get all excited . . . and then the next day, when I went to get it, it'd be gone. Really weird!

"But," he finished cheerfully, "as I say, so far, so good. Let's just hope our luck holds out this year."

"Could it be someone inside the camp who's responsible for those peculiar disappearances?" Susan wondered aloud. She was speaking more to herself than to the boy. "Someone who works here, maybe? Or even one of the campers?"

"Believe me, just about every possible theory has been considered. We've all even found ourselves wondering if we've been imagining some of this stuff! But," he said with a shrug, "no one's been able to come up with any solution.

"Anyway, as I said before, let's just hope this turns out to be one of Camp Pinewood's better years. The Reeds certainly deserve it . . . and frankly, I'm up for a good summer, too!"

Susan was encouraged by his optimism. "I certainly hope it works out that way. This is the first time I've ever done anything like this. . . ."

"Really? Then I hope you'll allow me to show you the ropes. And I guess a good place to start is to tell you my name. I'm Richard Thompson."

"I'm Susan Pratt. I must say," she went on, looking around at the huge, sunny arts and crafts room, "I'm quite impressed with all this."

"Wait until you see all the great supplies we've got to work with!"

For the next half hour, Susan and Richard took an informal inventory of the storage closet, exclaiming over the boxes of paints, crayons, and papers. In addition to the standard art supplies, there were pipe cleaners, paste, metallic papers . . . even bits of fabric.

"Wow, this stuff is great!" Susan exclaimed. "It's going to be so much fun, showing the kids how to work with all this! I just know they're going to love it!"

"You're really interested in art, aren't you?" Richard's tone was earnest.

"Well . . . yes. Aren't you?"

"Oh, definitely! It's just that it's hard to find people who are as serious about it as I am. Do you take art classes in school?"

It turned out that the two of them did indeed share a great love of art. While Susan's main interest was painting, Richard preferred sculpture.

They wiled away the rest of the morning, chatting enthusiastically about their favorite artists and styles. Richard planned to go on to art school after high school, just like Susan.

It wasn't until they heard the loud honk of what sounded like a bus, announcing its arrival, that they snapped back into the present.

"Goodness, what time is it?" Susan rushed to the window and saw that a blue school bus was trundling down the dirt driveway, toward the camp. It appeared to be filled with children, singing what she surmised must be the camp song.

"They're here!"

"We'd better get going, then," said Richard. "The way things were set up last year was that all the campers checked in at the dining hall first thing. They got their cabin assignments and were introduced to all the staff. Some of the counselors sleep in the cabins with the kids, you know. And the rest of us—well, we're what the Reeds consider 'specialists.' " Richard grinned. "We get our own cabins, and a lot more free time."

"I can't wait to meet the kids. Let's go over to the dining hall. And," Susan added as they packed away the last box of finger paints, "there's someone I want you to meet."

"You mean one of the campers?" Richard seemed puzzled.

"No, one of the other counselors. My sister."

"Oh."

"My *twin* sister."

"Oh! You mean there are *two* of you?" Richard chuckled.

"In appearance only. We're really quite different. But you'll find that out for yourself!"

As she and Richard started up the path leading from the arts and crafts building to the dining hall, Susan felt more optimistic about the summer ahead than she ever had before. The beautiful lake and woods, a bus filled with enthusiastic campers, a whole wealth of art supplies to work with . . . and a charming boy named Richard with whom to share the next six weeks. It was all turning out perfectly after all.

For now, the "ghosts" that haunted Camp Pinewood seemed very far away indeed.

Four

The twins' first full day at Camp Pinewood went well. The children all seemed so gleeful about being back at camp. Even the few who were already homesick allowed themselves to be cajoled out of their tearfulness with offers of a swim or the chance to ride in a canoe. Linda and Sam were eager to show their new cabinmates around. And, as Susan had predicted, Richard and Chris liked each other right off.

It was a long day, and by evening, Chris and Susan were both tired. But not too tired to go to the "Welcome" party that the Reeds always held for counselors on the first night of camp. Linda was also going, while Sam, tired out from a full day of nature walks, volunteered to be one of the counselors who stayed behind to keep an eye on the campers. Putting on sundresses and sandals for the occasion energized the twins, and by the time they walked over to the Reeds' house, they were already in a festive mood.

"Come on in, girls!" Mr. Reed, posted at the front door, greeted them heartily. "Help yourself to a glass of lemonade and some of those homemade cookies over there. Make yourselves at home!"

Surveying the twins carefully, he added, "I know you said that it was easy to tell you two apart . . . but for the life of me, I don't know which one's Chris and which one's Susan!"

The party was already well under way. Rock music played softly in the background, and some of the counselors were dancing in one corner of the living room. Laid out on the dining room table was a generous display of cold drinks, pretzels, and cookies. Somebody, probably Mrs. Reed, had obviously put in long hours of baking in order to make things special for the party.

Following Mr. Reed's advice, Susan went directly over to the refreshment table and helped herself to a glass of lemonade.

"Pretty thirsty, huh?"

She whirled around and found herself face to face with Richard.

"I guess this afternoon's session of making papier-mâché puppets with twenty-five eight-year-olds really took a lot out of you!"

"It *was* a long day," Susan admitted with a chuckle. "But I think it's turning out to be even more fun than I expected. For one thing, I'm finding out that *teaching* art is a lot different from *doing* art!"

"That's for sure. One major difference, I've found, is that doing it yourself is a lot less noisy!"

Armed with glasses of lemonade and some of

Mrs. Reed's homemade cookies, Susan and Richard ambled out to the porch that ran along the back of the house. It offered an unparalleled view of Lake Majestic. It was a clear night, and the moonlight reflecting off the waves was magnificent. Susan felt as if she had stepped into a picture postcard.

Chris, meanwhile, had been taken under Linda's wings. As a much more seasoned counselor, she already knew a lot of the other Camp Pinewood regulars. She introduced her around, and while Chris found it difficult to remember everyone's name, she could already tell that they were a great bunch. Before long, they were all talking and laughing together as a group, each one trying to outdo the others with humorous recollections of things that had happened in past years. The time that some of the kids put salt in all the sugar bowls, for example, and the annual water sports competition between the campers and the counselors.

After a while, Chris began to get the feeling that someone was staring at her. Her eyes automatically traveled to the door that led into the Reeds' kitchen. Alan Reed was standing there, looking as if he wanted to join the crowd but hesitating, probably out of shyness. But it was Chris he was watching.

She blushed, wondering why it was that he had singled her out. She had to admit that as uncomfortable as the boy made her feel, with his cold green staring eyes and stony silences, there was something intriguing about him. As she sat with the group of counselors, aware of his eyes upon her, she tried to tell herself that she simply felt sorry for him, since he seemed to be kind of a loner. But she couldn't help wondering if there was more to it.

Suddenly, she stood up and walked over to the refreshment table, pretending to want another cold drink. But the table also happened to be located right next to the kitchen door. As she casually poured herself a second glass of lemonade, she glanced over at Alan and smiled.

"Hello again," she said, trying to sound friendly.

"Hello."

The tall, lean boy looked a lot less forbidding than he had the first time she'd seen him. His straight black hair had been combed, and he was dressed in the same kind of T-shirt and khaki pants that most of the other boys were wearing. Most of all, the look in his eyes was much more open, without the guardedness she had seen in them the day before, when he had picked her up on the driveway.

He hesitated, then came over and helped himself to some lemonade. "It looks like everybody is having a good time." He gestured toward the crowd in the living room, still laughing together about the funnier moments in Camp Pinewood's history. Chris noticed that Richard and Susan had just come in from outside to join them.

"Yes," she agreed. "And from what I can tell, it also looks like everybody really enjoys working here at Camp Pinewood. Listening to them makes me glad that I'm here. I feel as if I'm lucky to be part of all this."

"That's a shame." Alan's voice had become bitter, and that same icy look she had seen before had come into his eyes again. "I hate to disappoint you and everybody else, but I'm afraid that at the moment the future of Camp Pinewood looks kind of dismal."

"So I've heard."

"I wish I could be as carefree as they all are tonight," he went on, staring off at the crowd of counselors but seeming not to really see them.

There was an awkward silence. Chris broke it, her voice strangely high-pitched from its forced cheerfulness. "Well, I guess I'll go back to the others. I see my sister just reappeared. I thought she'd gotten lost. . . ."

"I'm sorry," Alan said suddenly, his voice softer. "I didn't mean to sound so angry. Or to lay my family's problems on you. Please don't just walk away."

"O-okay." Chris was surprised by this sudden change. She was also surprised to see this other side of Alan Reed that was suddenly emerging. *And* curious to know more about it.

"Why don't we go outside on the porch?" he suggested. "It'll be much quieter there. Besides, there's a full moon out tonight. You should see how beautiful Lake Majestic looks.

"So, you live in Whittington," Alan said as they leaned against the porch railing, taking in the view and sipping their lemonade. "That's about a hundred fifty miles from here, isn't it?"

"Why, yes, it is." Chris was surprised. "How did you know where I'm from?"

"Oh, I just happened to check out your application. I figure it can't hurt to know something about the people who work for my folks." He tried to keep his voice light, but it was obvious to Chris that Alan didn't bother to "research" all of the counselors.

"What else do you know about me?"

"Not too much. But I hope to find out more."

His last remark really startled her. And here she'd thought he was staring at her from across the room because he didn't like her!

"Well, of the two of us, I'd say that *you're* the mysterious one, Alan Reed! You seem so distant . . . as if you're a thousand miles away."

"Yeah, I know. The truth is, I have been pretty preoccupied lately. Worried about the camp, and my parents, too.

"But tonight is supposed to be a night for celebrating, not worrying! We've got the whole summer ahead of us. Besides, I shouldn't be burdening you with my family's problems, anyway. Hey—I have an idea. Are you in a daring mood tonight?"

"Pretty daring . . . Why?"

"How about a moonlight swim?"

"Well . . ."

"Come on. We'll just slip away, and no one will ever even notice that we're gone. I know I'm in good hands, since you are the swimming instructor and all. Having you there is even safer than inviting along a lifeguard! Besides, you've got to admit that Lake Majestic looks pretty inviting!"

Chris laughed. "You certainly can be convincing! All right, it sounds like fun. Let me go change into a suit, and I'll meet you at the boathouse as soon as I can."

"You're on!"

Fifteen minutes later, the two of them were splashing around in the lake, laughing like children who were doing something they weren't really supposed to be doing. Unwinding in the cool, refreshing water was the perfect ending to the first day of camp.

"Maybe we'd better get back to the party, before anyone misses us," Chris said after a while. "I wouldn't want to hurt your parents' feelings."

"Don't you think they'll notice that their son and their swimming instructor both have unusually wet hair?" Alan grinned.

"Oh, you're right! I guess that's the end of that party." Chris sat cross-legged on the dock, wrapped in the towel she'd brought along. She did feel bad about deserting the party . . . but at the same time, she was having a wonderful time. Her swim had revitalized her, it was lovely sitting out by the moonlit lake . . . and Alan Reed, much to her continued surprise, was turning out to be excellent company.

"Since you're the one who dragged me away from all those homemade cookies, I'd say the very least you can do is tell me all about yourself."

"There's not much to tell." Alan shrugged. "During the summers, I work here. During the year, I go to high school. I'll be a senior next year. I'm on the basketball team and the school newspaper, my best subject is science, and I enjoy learning about nature. In fact, I'm really looking forward to Camp Pinewood's first annual outing next Tuesday."

Chris was puzzled. "I don't remember hearing about any outing."

"It's always one of the hits of the summer. We're taking the ten-year-olds to a local wildlife preserve. We pack them up with box lunches, load them onto the big blue bus, and lead them on a full day of exploring the nature preserve. It's always one of the highlights of my vacation."

"It sounds like fun. I don't suppose you can find a place for a swimming instructor. . . ."

Alan laughed. "I'm afraid you'll have to stay here and entertain all the other kids, those who aren't lucky enough to come along.

"Now, if I don't get into some warm, dry clothes soon, I think I may turn into a snowman! Unfortunately, I didn't have the foresight to bring along a towel!"

"I guess these moonlight swims are not part of your normal schedule," Chris teased. "But it *is* getting chilly, now that you mention it. Even with this towel that I had the 'foresight' to bring along, I'm getting cold. I'd better go back to my cabin and change, too."

"Okay. I'll walk you back."

"Afraid I'll get lost in the dark?"

"I could certainly use that as an excuse," said Alan. "After all, I know these rocky paths a lot better than you do. Or I could just be honest and say that I'm having such a good time that I don't want the evening to end yet."

"Well, that's hard to argue with. Especially since I feel exactly the same way!"

Arm in arm, Chris and Alan began the uphill climb from the lake to the cabins. They were laughing loudly, wrapped up in their joy over having found someone they could have so much fun with.

They never even suspected that they were being watched.

Five

The morning of the ten-year-olds' outing to the Lake Majestic Wildlife Preserve, a sprawling national park over on the other side of the lake, Jake Reed awoke with the feeling that it was going to turn out to be a perfect day. The sun was shining brightly, its heat tempered by the cool breeze that wafted off the lake. The bus was all checked out and ready to go; the afternoon before, he and Alan had spent several hours working on the motor, anxious to make sure that the first outing of the camp season proceeded smoothly. And probably most important, the campers themselves were excited. Although camp had only been in session for a little more than a week, Samantha and the other nature counselors had already given them a good background in birds, trees, and flowers—exactly the kind of thing they would be seeing at the wildlife preserve.

Jake was whistling as he strode out of the house, waving to Alan, who was up ahead, near the bus. But as soon as he saw the expression on his son's face, his whistling stopped.

"Oh, no!" he cried. "What is it this time, Alan?"

"Somebody decided we could make the trip without air in our tires," Alan said grimly, gesturing toward the bus.

Sure enough, the air had been let out of all four of the tires. Not just a little, either; every one of them was completely flat. The sight of the tremendous blue bus standing by the side of the road on four flabby black tires might have been comical if it hadn't been for the fact that the mere sight of it made Jake Reed's stomach tighten.

"Well, we'll just have to get the hand pump and start pumping."

"That'll take at least an hour. It's almost eight, and we told the kids we'd be leaving at eight-thirty on the dot."

"We'll just have to explain that we need to make a few repairs on the bus before we can get going." Jake tried to sound matter-of-fact, but he knew as well as Alan that such a delay—especially where something as exciting as an outing to a wildlife preserve was concerned—was exactly the kind of thing that would be reported to parents immediately, in letters and telephone calls home.

"I'll get the pump," Alan offered. "But first I'll tell Mom to alert the counselors. Maybe they can come up with some way to distract a few dozen disappointed ten-year-olds."

At nine o'clock, Alan and his father were still pumping up the last tire. The campers started arriving, led by their counselors, chattering away excitedly as they anticipated the journey ahead. They'd already been looking forward to it for days. They were armed with binoculars, box lunches, and sweaters.

"Just in time," muttered Jake. "I'd hate to have to tell this crowd that we still weren't ready for 'em."

Alan shared his father's relief. As he watched the campers pile onto the bus, he told himself that a half-hour delay was really nothing to get upset about. He watched from the side of the road, expecting to see his father drive away with a busload of cheering kids.

But as his father went to start the engine, it resisted, offering little besides a pessimistic whirring sound.

Something else was wrong.

Immediately Alan sprang into action. Within seconds he was poking around the motor, trying to find out what was going on.

"Just another minute or so, kids," he heard his father call to the campers with false heartiness. "We'll have this big blue machine moving in no time!"

It took Alan a few minutes to figure out what had happened. At first, it looked as if everything was in order. He was puzzled. But then he checked under the distributor cap—not a place it would ordinarily occur to him to look—and discovered that the rotor was missing. Someone had taken it.

"Dad, could I talk to you a minute?" He tried to keep the fury out of his voice.

"Just a second, kids. I think Alan's found out what the problem is."

"I found the problem, all right," he said angrily, once his father had come closer, out of earshot of the children. "Someone stole the rotor."

Jake sighed heavily. "They probably didn't steal it—just hid it someplace cute, like in the refrigerator or underneath the front porch. Well, kids or no kids, I guess the only thing for us to do is drive the pickup into town and get a new rotor. Rudy's opens at nine, doesn't it?"

"I'll go," Alan volunteered.

But as soon as he got near the pickup, parked on the other side of the house, he stopped dead in his tracks.

The air had been let out of all four of the truck's tires, as well.

He felt like stomping around and yelling and then going out to find the person who was responsible for all this. But he couldn't. So instead, he went back to his father, who was explaining to the busload of wailing ten-year-olds that their departure would have to be postponed once again—for at least another hour.

"Better make that two hours, Dad," Alan muttered. "It looks like the pickup isn't going anywhere, either. At least until we take the time to pump up *its* tires, too."

Jake Reed shook his head slowly. "We'd better cancel the trip altogether. For today, anyway. Do you want to be the one to break the news to sixty eager kids who are already jumping out of their skins, or should I?"

By lunchtime, the entire camp was buzzing about the morning's canceled trip to the Lake Majestic Wildlife Preserve. True, it had been rescheduled for the following week. But to the ten-year-olds who had been all ready to go, the following week seemed very far away indeed. And all the other campers were sympathetic. They knew how disappointed they would have been if it had been they who were counting on a trip. And even though they understood all about the broken bus and pickup truck, they couldn't help blaming it all on the staff of Camp Pinewood.

"I'm going to tell my mother and father about this," said Lucy Kramer, one of the camp's more outspoken ten-year-olds. She had just sat down at one of the long dining room tables. To help reverse the somber mood that had fallen over the camp, the Reeds had ordered the kitchen staff to prepare a special lunch. And Lucy had certainly taken advantage of it. Her tray was piled high with french fries and chocolate cake—and little else besides.

"I've been waiting to go to the wildlife preserve ever since I got here. I even brought my father's binoculars, especially for something like this! And now we have to stay around this stupid old camp all day. Boy, I'm going to write my parents a letter about this right after lunch. And they're going to be plenty mad!"

Chris, sitting behind her at the next table, couldn't help overhearing the little girl's tirade.

"I have a better idea, Lucy," she said gently. It took everything she had to keep the anger out of her voice. "Go ahead and write to your parents and tell them that the trip to the wildlife preserve was canceled at the last minute because of some trouble the Reeds were having with the camp's bus. But instead of complaining about it, why don't you tell them that while you were disappointed at first, you decided that it would be babyish to let it ruin your day? Tell them that instead you realized that things don't always work out exactly the way we want, and that you're determined to make the best of it. And that now, you even have something extra special to look forward to for next week!"

The little girl was dumbfounded at first. Then a smile crept over her face slowly. "You know, that might not be such a bad idea. Maybe my parents will even send me a *present* when they hear how grown-up I'm acting!"

"Now *that's* what I call fast thinking!" said Alan, who happened to be walking by. "How'd you like a job as the official Public Relations director of Camp Pinewood? We could use a few more people with your sense of diplomacy!" He sat down at the table, across from her.

Chris blushed at his compliment. "Well, you've got to admit that Lucy *was* being a bit childish. From what I've heard around the dining room, I don't think most of the kids are taking it quite so hard."

"I hope not. But this is exactly the kind of thing that's been happening around here over the past couple of summers. We look like we don't know what we're doing—usually because of some stupid little thing. Harmless, too, except that it ends up creating a lot of bad feeling. Sometimes I wonder if even the counselors realize it's not our fault."

"Alan, I just got an idea."

"At this point, I'm open to absolutely anything."

"Why don't you *tell* the counselors it's not your fault?"

"What do you mean? I just assumed . . ."

"I know. I've been assuming the same thing. But maybe it wouldn't be such a bad idea to hold a meeting with all the counselors and explain things to them. It's true that everyone seems aware that something is happening . . . but it's all based on rumors. Or second- or even third-hand accounts. I think everyone would feel better if it were more out in the open. Besides," she added, hoping she wasn't stepping out of line, "it might help things if you could give some of us counselors some advice on how to deal with the kids' confusion about all this."

"You mean the way you just did."

"Well . . . yes, sort of. I'm not saying I'm an expert or anything, but . . ."

"You've made your point," Alan laughed. His green eyes were no longer clouded. "And I think it's a great idea. How about right after lunch? Think that's too soon?"

"I think it's the perfect time. Especially since all the kids will be going back to their cabins now for Quiet Hour. That gives the counselors a chance to stay around for a while."

Once lunch was over and the campers had gone back to their sleeping quarters to rest, read, or write letters home, Alan stood up in front of the counselors who had stayed behind in the dining hall at his request.

"As most of you already know, we had a bit of a problem with Camp Pinewood's advanced transportation system this morning. The trip to the Lake Majestic Wildlife Preserve had to be canceled at the last minute. As of right now, there are a lot of very disappointed ten-years-old wandering around these parts.

"But I think you should all know that what

happened this morning was no accident. And it wasn't the result of carelessness or poor planning or any of those things. The truth is, it appears that someone is trying to sabotage Camp Pinewood.''

"Whatever for?" asked one of the new counselors.

"That," Alan replied grimly, "is something we haven't been able to determine."

"And who's responsible?" asked Linda. "I mean, a lot of us have had an idea of what's been going on for a long time now. But what we can't figure out is who's behind it."

"Another good question," said Alan. "And, I might add, something else we'd like to find out. Unfortunately, neither my parents nor I have been able to come up with any answers. . . ."

Chris, sitting in the back, was watching and listening sadly. Now that she was experiencing the "mysterious goings-on" firsthand, she could see how frustrating it all was. And how destructive to the morale of Camp Pinewood—and the Reeds.

She searched the crowd until she found Susan. She was right in front, listening carefully to everything Alan was saying. And knowing her twin, Chris suspected that she was as concerned as she was.

Well, one thing's for sure, thought Chris. I'm not going to stand by and just let all this happen. *Somebody* has to get to the bottom of it. And if anyone can do it, it's Sooz and me!

Six

That evening, right after dinner, Chris and Susan found themselves alone in their cabin. Sam was giving a special nature lecture, and Linda was off for a swim with some friends. The twins were lounging across their beds, Susan lying sprawled out, Chris sitting cross-legged.

It was the perfect time, Chris decided, to talk to her twin.

"So, Sooz," she said casually, "we've been at Camp Pinewood for over a week now. What do you think so far?"

"So far, I'd have to say that coming here was one of the best ideas anyone in our family ever came up with. I love the kids, and it's fun teaching them all about color and how to use all the neat supplies we've got packed away in the storeroom." Susan stretched her arms lazily. "The lake is beautiful; the other counselors are nice, especially Sam and Linda. . . . Even the food is good."

"You left out one thing!" Chris teased.

"What?"

"Does the name 'Richard Thompson' ring a bell?"

"Oh, Richard." Susan blushed. "Well, we do have a lot in common, since we both like art so much. . . ."

"Really? Is that what you two were talking about out on the porch, at the Reeds' 'Welcome' party? In the moonlight, I might add?"

"Seems to me I noticed you and Alan Reed disappearing out onto that same porch." Susan grinned. "In that same moonlight!"

"Well, we had things to talk about."

"Oh, I see. Comparing notes on favorite swimming techniques?"

Chris suddenly grew serious. "As a matter of fact, I wanted to talk to you about Alan." She began toying with the shoelace of her sneaker.

"Oooh, this sounds juicy." Susan propped herself up on one elbow. Her brown eyes glowed mischievously. "I had a feeling there was something going on between you two. But I wasn't quite sure. . . ."

"Frankly, I'm not sure, either. But that's not what I wanted to talk to you about."

It was then that Susan noticed how serious her twin had become.

"What is it, Chris?" Suddenly, she was concerned.

"It's all the peculiar things that have been happening around Camp Pinewood."

"Oh. Like what happened this morning. Gee, that was creepy. Someone letting all the air out of the tires of the bus and the pickup on the very day the kids were scheduled to take a field trip." Susan shuddered. "It's pretty awful, isn't it? I mean, we knew those things had happened, from what the Reeds and the other counselors said. But somehow, experiencing it firsthand like that . . . well, it really gave me the creeps."

"I know exactly what you mean, Sooz. Imagine, someone's sneaking around, doing all these mean, destructive things. And the worst part is, whoever's doing it seems to know exactly what's going on here at the camp! Like the fact that that trip was scheduled for today, of all days."

Susan thought for a minute. "Do you think that the person responsible works here, Chris? That maybe one of the counselors—or even one of the campers—is behind it all?"

"I don't know, Sooz. But there's one thing I *do* know."

"What's that?"

"That you and I are going to get to the bottom of this."

"You and I?" Susan nearly fell off the bed.

"That's right," her twin replied calmly.

"But Chris! What can *we* possibly do? We don't know anything about all this. I wouldn't know where to begin! Why, most of the other counselors, and even some of the kids, know more about Camp Pinewood than you and I do. They've been coming here for years! And then there are the Reeds. They *own* the camp, for heaven's sake, and even they can't figure out what's going on!"

"I know all that, Sooz. But I can't just sit back and watch this happen! You can see what it's doing to Mr. and Mrs. Reed! And Alan, too, of course." Her voice had become pleading.

"Yes, it is sad, isn't it? And I do feel kind of helpless," Susan confessed. "Like there must be *something* I can do to help."

"Exactly. Besides, you and I have never been afraid to take on challenges like this before. What about those times we traded places? You've got to admit that that was a pretty daring thing to do, too."

"Yes . . . But where do we start, Chris?"

Chris was staring off into space, lost in thought. "To be perfectly honest, I don't know the answer to that yet. But I'm working on it. All I want from you right now is your commitment to helping me. To helping the Reeds."

Another thought suddenly occurred to Susan. "Chris, do you think this could be dangerous?"

"Dangerous?"

"The people we're dealing with, I mean. After all, it could turn out to be a lot more serious than just some of the campers playing practical jokes that aren't turning out to be very funny."

Chris looked at her twin. "I don't know, Sooz. I really don't. But I think it's up to us to find out. Are you with me?"

Susan had never seen her sister so earnest about anything before in all their sixteen years. It was clear that this was very, very important to her.

She wasn't about to let her sister down.

"All right, Chris," she said with the same seriousness. "You've got yourself a partner!"

With Susan's agreement that something simply had to be done—and that the Pratt twins were the ones to do it—Chris was in a good mood once again. Having decided to do something about the situation, to take action, made her feel optimistic. The fact that she had no idea *what* she was going to do didn't even seem that important, at least for the moment.

Susan, on the other hand, was still doubtful. While she agreed that some action needed to be taken, she wondered if she and Chris were really the ones to be doing it. Aside from that was the obvious question, What could they do? Where could they start? Certainly her twin meant well, and she was willing to do whatever she could. But taking on the "phantom" of Camp Pinewood seemed like an awfully ambitious project.

Later that evening, at the campfire sing-along, Richard picked up on Susan's pensive mood right away.

"Is this an example of artistic temperament?" he teased, sitting down next to her, cross-legged. He was wearing a plaid flannel shirt and blue jeans, and with his sandy hair and blue eyes, he reminded her of a lumberjack. "You look as if you're a million miles away."

"Maybe I'm working on getting some inspiration," she returned with a laugh. "I didn't even realize I was daydreaming."

"Here, I've got the perfect cure for uncontrollable woolgathering." He produced a bag of marshmallows and two long wooden sticks that had been stripped of their branches.

"Toasted marshmallows! What a great idea! I haven't had any of these for ages—not since *I* was a camper myself. Wherever did you get them?"

"I'm afraid I can't take full credit. The Reeds are handing them out, over there. I *did* hand-craft these magnificent marshmallow-toasters from simple branches, however. Observe the clean lines, the streamlined top. . . . One of the more practical applications of my artistic abilities!"

"I knew right from the start that you were a valuable person to know."

"I hope you really mean that, Susan." Richard suddenly sounded much more serious. "And I hope it's more than my marshmallow-toasting abilities that are making you feel that way."

When Susan looked over at him, she could tell, even by firelight, that his cheeks were turning pink.

"I'm well aware that there's more to Richard Thompson than just a talented artist and an expert marshmallow-toaster," she said gently.

When they both agreed that eating even one more marshmallow would be impossible, Susan suggested that they take a walk.

"Come on. Let's stretch our legs. After being inside all day, I need some exercise."

"What? You mean you don't consider twisting colored pipe cleaners into giraffes and elephants and assorted fuzzy monsters good exercise?"

Once they were away from the others, strolling hand in hand by the lake's shore, Susan grew serious once again.

"You know, Richard, there's a reason why I looked like I was a million miles away before."

"Really? What's on your mind?"

"Well, I had a heart-to-heart talk with my sister."

"Oh? Then what's on Chris's mind?"

Susan frowned. "She's really concerned about the Reeds and the problems they've been having with Camp Pinewood."

"Are you sure her interest in all this doesn't have

something to do with the Reeds' son?'' Richard smiled knowingly. "It seems to me that I've noticed some longing gazes between the two of them."

"Maybe it's related, a little bit. But that's not important. What matters is that she's determined to find out who's responsible for all the strange things that have been going on. To get to the bottom of this."

"Sounds like a noble gesture."

"Well . . . yes, I suppose it is. It's just that she wants me to help her. I'd like to help, of course," Susan added quickly. "I'm just afraid this might be a little out of my league. Hers, too, for that matter."

"If it helps any, Susan, I have every confidence that you can do it."

"You do?" Susan gulped.

"Yes. As a matter of fact . . ." Richard stopped walking and turned to face her. Gently he placed his hands on her waist and drew her closer to him. "I have a feeling that you're someone who can do anything in the world she wants, once she sets her mind to it."

Susan could hardly breathe. And her heart was pounding so fiercely that she was certain he could hear it. But if he could, he didn't seem to care. Instead, he was looking at her so intensely, his eyes locked in hers, that she felt as if no one were around for miles. All she was aware of was the moonlight, the lapping of the lake's waves, and Richard.

"Yes," he said softly, "I think you're pretty special, Susan Pratt."

When he leaned forward and kissed her, Susan suddenly forgot all about the moonlight and the lake.

Seven

The annual counselors' show was one of the biggest events of every Camp Pinewood season. It was always held at the beginning of the third week. That way, the campers already knew most of the counselors and could appreciate seeing them perform on the outdoor "stage" that was set up behind the dining hall. Yet it was still early enough so that for the rest of the summer the campers and counselors could tease one another about it, singing the songs that were used in the show and calling the counselors by the nicknames that inevitably grew out of the one-and-only performance.

There was no fixed format for the show, and every year it was different. One thing that remained the same, however, was that all the planning was done by the counselors. The play itself, the costumes and makeup and sets, even the musical instruments that were used to accompany the hearty singing that always seemed to be included, were all created with whatever ingenuity and miscellaneous odds and ends the counselors could scrounge up. And the fact that they had only a very short time in which to do it all lent an extra air of excitement to the project.

"Let's call this meeting to order!" Linda, the voluntary director of this year's show, had to shout in order to be heard among the crowd of chattering counselors. They had all gathered together in the dining hall for their first planning session. They all had their own ideas and were anxious to tell them to anyone who was willing to listen. Chris and Susan sat in the back wth Richard, marveling over the amount of noise that such a modest-size group could manage to make.

"As you all know," Linda began, "for all of us counselors here at Camp Pinewood, this is our one chance to shine. To taste stardom. And, in some cases, to make utter fools of ourselves!"

Everyone laughed. They realized that that was part of the fun of the counselors' show.

"Now, we all have a lot of work to do. But before we can get started, we have to decide what *kind* of show we want to have. Any suggestions?"

"How about a musical?" Sam suggested from the side of the room, where she was sitting with some of the other nature counselors. "We could write an entirely original play and then write our own songs to go with it."

"Or we could use *real* songs," piped up one of the boating instructors. "Songs everyone knows already. From the radio."

"That would certainly make things easier,"

Linda agreed. "Unless we have some budding composers out there . . . Susan, I see you have your hand up. Are you volunteering to become our resident songwriter?"

"I think painting sets would be more my speed," Susan chuckled. She stood up so she could be heard. "Actually, I have an idea for the show that might be a little bit different from what I understand has been done in other years."

"We're open to all kinds of suggestions."

Susan took a deep breath. "Well, how about a variety show? That way, we'll all have the chance to do what we do best—no matter what that might be. Singing, dancing, even reciting a poem. Everybody can be in it."

In response to her suggestion, the counselors began chattering away again. Linda held up her hands for silence.

"You're right, Susan. I don't think that's been done before. At least not that I know of."

"That's true; it hasn't been done before," boomed a voice from the doorway at the back of the dining hall. Everyone turned to see Alan Reed striding in. "I hope you don't mind me crashing your meeting like this, but, well, the truth is, I was curious. I've been watching the counselors' shows ever since I was a little kid, and I have yet to see how one of them comes about."

"You're welcome to join us," said Linda. "And it sounds like you've got some helpful background information that could help us out."

"Well, as I say, we've never had a variety show before. That's my official report, as a relative of the camp's owners." Alan grinned. "If you'd like an unofficial report on my opinion, as an objective observer, I think it's a great idea!"

"Let's take a vote," Sam suggested.

"All right. We can decide to have a variety show right now, or we can continue to discuss all the possibilities. All in favor of going ahead with a variety show, raise your hands. . . ."

It was unanimous; everyone thought the variety show was an excellent idea.

"I had no idea you had a flair for the theater!" whispered Richard, giving Susan's hand a squeeze.

"Good work, Sooz!" her twin said a second later.

"But now I have to come up with an idea for an act!" Susan moaned. "I think I outsmarted myself!"

An hour or so later, after the meeting was over, she was still agonizing over what kind of act she could put together—and in just a few days. As Richard walked the twins back to their cabin, the three of them were trying to think of something unusual that they could do in the show.

"I can't sing, I can't dance, and I don't know a single poem!" Chris wailed. "Susan Pratt, what have you gotten us into?"

"Well, I'm no better off," countered her sister. "Unless I ask for volunteers from the audience and sketch their portraits, right on the spot."

Chris groaned. "An impressive ability, my dear twin. But hardly the stuff that opening nights are made of."

"I have an idea," said Richard. "It's an act that all three of us could do together. It would require some planning, of course, and a lot of practice. But none of us would have to sing or dance or any of that stuff. And, I might add, it could well turn out to be the hit of the show."

"It sounds perfect!" Chris exclaimed. "I'm willing to agree to it, here and now, without knowing anything more than what you just told us!"

As usual, her sister was more cautious. "I don't know. It sounds almost too good to be true. What's the trick?"

"The trick, my dear, is originality. That, coupled with the fact that I happen to have the good fortune to be teamed up with a pair of identical twins."

"Oooh, I think I'm beginning to like this idea even more." Chris's brown eyes twinkled mischievously. "Fooling people about which one of us is which happens to be one of my favorite hobbies. Not to mention one of our specialties."

"Here's the idea: we'll do a magic act."

"A magic act! How clever!" cried Susan.

"I'll be the magician, and we'll pretend that one of you—*only* one of you—is my assistant. In fact," Richard went on thoughtfully, "we could even start a rumor that the other twin is in the infirmary. That would *really* help our act!"

"But I don't understand," Chris said impatiently. "What's the gimmick?"

"The gimmick is that you'd *both* be part of the act. In the magic tricks we did we'd take advantage of the fact that you two look the same."

Susan looked puzzled. "I'm afraid I still don't get it."

"Well, for example, I could have my 'assistant' climb into a big box, right on stage, in clear view of everybody. I'd wave my magic wand over the box, claiming I was going to make her disappear. The box would have a false bottom, of course, and whoever was inside would simply climb underneath, out of sight. When I opened the box, it would be empty.

"But that's only the first part of the trick. A few seconds later, the *other* twin, dressed the same as my assistant, would appear from the side of the stage! The kids will be flabbergasted!"

"And they'll never figure out how we did it, either!" Susan was growing excited. "Especially if they think one of us is stashed away in the infirmary!"

"Oh, let's do it!" cried Chris. "I think it's a fantastic idea!"

"Okay. I'm glad you two are so enthusiastic. Now we have to put our heads together and come up with some more magic acts that use your identical appearances."

"And plan the props we'll need . . . and build them . . ."

"And come up with some kind of costumes."

"But I love the idea!" said Susan. "And I think you were right, Richard. Our act *is* going to be the hit of the show!"

For the next few days, Chris and Susan and Richard spent every spare moment working on their act. They dyed an old sheet black and sewed on big gold stars to create a magician's cape. Chris and Susan put together identical outfits for the "assistants" to wear—red shorts and white T-shirts, printed in red with the Camp Pinewood insignia. And the three of them, working together, thought up half a dozen magic tricks. Some were simple, using a white stuffed rabbit they borrowed from one of the campers and a bouquet of paper flowers that Susan made from the colored crêpe paper she found in the art supply closet. But some used the twins' identical appearances—like the very first one that Richard had come up with, the one that had convinced them to go ahead with his idea.

The campers, aware that all the counselors were busy planning for the counselors' show, were also getting excited. As the number of days until the big event got smaller and smaller, the entire camp began to buzz with anticipation.

As always, Jake Reed and his son were prepared to do everything they could to make the evening memorable. They built the stage behind the dining hall—little more than a simple platform, really, with two panels blocking off the backstage area. But the counselors decorated it with crêpe paper streamers, balloons, and more of Susan's handmade flowers. And under Susan's direction they painted an elaborate backdrop, a colorful conglomeration of bold colors and shapes. A few of the counselors even fashioned a simple curtain out of sheets. Everyone agreed that this year's stage was the best one the camp had ever had.

Aside from the stage, Jake arranged to rent dozens of wooden folding chairs for the audience to sit in. This, too, was part of Camp Pinewood's tradition. This one night was designed to be extra special, and no effort was spared.

Finally, it was Friday, the day of the counselors' show. The stage had been completed, the chairs had been delivered and stored until evening in one of the sheds on the edge of the camp grounds, and the last finishing touches had been put on the different acts. It was a beautiful day, sunny but cool, and the weather report promised that the delightful weather would hold up through the evening. Everything seemed to be proceeding smoothly.

That evening's performance was the only thing that anyone talked about all day. Susan even had difficulty maintaining order during her arts and crafts sessions. The kids were unusually restless, keyed up over the upcoming event. They weren't interested in paints or clay or pipe cleaners. All they wanted to do was talk about the show.

"I haven't even *looked* at the stage yet," declared Lucy Kramer. "I know everyone else has, but *I* want to be surprised."

"Not me," chimed in Maggie, one of her friends. "I've been watching every step. I'm even bringing my camera tonight. I want to take pictures of the stage, and the chairs all set up . . . just like a *real* theater!"

"Except that it's outside," Lucy said proudly. "I bet there's no other theater in the world like ours!"

"I'm glad you're all looking forward to tonight," said Susan. "Now, how about if we get out some crayons, and draw? . . ."

"But I don't *want* to draw!" Lucy pouted. "Nobody else does, either. Can't we talk about the show? Tell us about it, Susan. You know all about it, since you're in it, aren't you?"

"Yes, I am. All the counselors are in the show." Craftily, she added, "Except for my twin sister, Chris. You all know Chris, don't you? The swimming instructor?"

"How come she's not in it?" asked Maggie.

"Because she's sick. In fact, she's in the infirmary right now. Poor Chris won't even be able to watch the show, much less be in it."

"That's too bad," said Maggie.

"Yes, it is." Susan smiled to herself.

There, she had done it. She had started the rumor that Chris was in the infirmary, tucked out of the way.

Suddenly she came up with a brainstorm. "Hey, I've got an idea. How about if today, instead of painting or drawing, everyone makes a costume to wear to the counselors' show? We have fabric, and crêpe paper, and ribbons. . . . And I can teach you how to make paper flowers and hats and funny jewelry. How about it?"

Susan wasn't at all surprised by the cry of glee that rose up from the group.

Two hours before the show was scheduled to begin, Alan Reed drove the pickup truck out to the storage shed. He'd wanted to bring the chairs over to the stage earlier, to make sure he had time to get them all set up. But he'd been so busy all day that this was the first chance he'd gotten. Now he was really going to have to hurry if he wanted to finish on time.

Like everyone else, he was looking forward to seeing the counselors' show. It was too bad about Chris . . . but he would report to her every single detail he could remember, right after it was over. Ordinarily, visiting hours at the infirmary didn't extend so late, but tonight was a special occasion.

He had a feeling that for once, the nurse over there would make an exception.

Alan was whistling as he opened up the door of the shed. He hadn't noticed before how worn the wooden bolt was. He made a mental note to put on a new one the very first thing in the morning. Why, this one was barely keeping the door closed, much less discouraging anyone from sneaking in and rummaging around.

"Well, this is going to be one big job," he muttered, going inside. The mere thought of lugging dozens of heavy wooden folding chairs out onto the pickup and hoisting them up on back made him tired.

But as he walked into the dark shed, his stomach suddenly sank.

All the chairs were gone.

Eight

"Ladies and gentlemen, boys and girls, Camp Pinewood campers—and anyone else who might be out there. Welcome to the counselors' variety show!"

At last, it was time for the long-awaited spectacle to begin.

Samantha Collier, the mistress of ceremonies, had just stepped onto the stage, dressed in an "evening gown" fashioned from spangles and glitter and fabric found in the arts and crafts building's magical storage closet. Her blond hair was festooned with ribbons, and her makeup was exaggerated: red lips, pink cheeks, huge black eyelashes painted on above her eyes.

The stage looked magnificent, with its garlands of paper flowers and other decorations. The set that Susan had designed was in place; the lighting was ready; costumes and makeup had been donned. The performers stayed hidden behind the wooden partitions on both sides of the stage, waiting excitedly for their turn. Any last-minute stage fright was rapidly being replaced by a sense of excitement. Finally, after long preparation, it was showtime. This was it!

The only thing that was less than perfect was the fact that the entire audience was sitting on the grass—instead of on the folding wooden chairs they had all been expecting. At first, many of them were disappointed over their discovery that one of the special touches of the evening was nowhere in sight.

"Hey, where are all the chairs?" Lucy Kramer asked loudly, stopping in her tracks. "I thought this was supposed to look like a *real* theater."

"Does this mean we have to sit on the *ground*?" whined her sidekick, Maggie. "But I'm wearing my brand-new shorts! I don't want to sit on the ground! My shorts will get all *dirty*!"

Fortunately, most of the other campers got over their initial surprise with more ease—and less resentment.

"Who cares?" countered Tim Tinker, one of the twelve-year-olds. "Just as long as we can see the stage, what difference does it make where we sit?"

"Yeah," agreed Eleanor Cousins, another twelve-year-old. "You girls make it sound as if you've never sat on the grass before. Isn't being outdoors the whole idea of going to camp?"

Chris, overhearing their conversation, was relieved that most of the campers seemed to take the change in plans in stride. As she watched the final touches being put on the stage from her hiding place in the arts and crafts building, then saw the campers beginning to assemble in front of it at a few minutes before seven, she, too, began to wonder what had happened to the chairs.

But then Alan walked by, unaware that he was being watched.

As soon as she saw his face, she knew there was something wrong. It was something more than an error on the rental company's part, or someone's forgetfulness in ordering the right thing for the right night. It was that same peculiar thing that had been going on for so long. Again. Things disappearing. Things going wrong. All for no good reason, nothing that could be explained.

Chris wanted to rush over to Alan, to find out exactly what had happened, to say something that might make him feel a little better. But she couldn't—not now. Not unless she was willing to ruin the act she and Susan and Richard had put so much hard work into.

I'll just have to talk to Alan later, she thought, watching him sadly. He glanced at the mass of campers gathering on the grass, shook his head slowly, and disappeared into the Reeds' house, looking as if he had lost interest in even watching the show.

But as far as Chris was concerned, she had to make herself forget all about Alan for now. The show must go on! Anxious to make her performance the very best she possibly could—partly to help the campers forget about everything except what a good time they were having—she resolved to concentrate only on their magic act until the show was over.

Their act, judged to be the best in the show, was being saved for last. That meant that Chris had a whole evening's entertainment ahead of her, as a spectator. From her vantage point at the side window of the arts and crafts building, she had an excellent view of the stage. And she could hear just about everything that was going on.

The acts in the variety show were as different as Camp Pinewood's counselors themselves. There were singers, mimes, and musicians. A boy and a girl did an energetic tap dance; another girl, who'd been studying ballet ever since she was six years old, did a short dance from *Swan Lake*. One group of four put on a comical skit about life at Camp Pinewood. And a spirited threesome played a medley of songs on kazoos, guitar, and garbage pail drums.

The costumes were as inspired as the acts themselves. Considering the fact that no one had actually brought anything along with them to camp—with the exception of ballet and tap shoes—it was impressive to see the effects that had been created with bathing suits and sheets, feathers and makeup, lengths of fabric and funny hats.

The counselors were all good performers, with some of the least likely blossoming into real hams once they were in the spotlight. They all seemed to be having a good time. More important, the campers loved the show. They laughed and cheered and applauded all the way through, their interest held by the constantly changing cast of characters on the stage. Even Lucy Kramer appeared to be enjoying herself, if the amount of time she spent jumping up and down and squealing at the end of each performance was any measure.

Chris was enjoying herself so much that she almost forgot that she, too, would eventually be called up on the stage. She was totally absorbed in watching each act. But as the trio of makeshift musicians was finishing up, she noticed something peculiar out of the corner of her eye. Automatically she looked over to the left. It was past eight by then, and the dense trees covering so much of Camp Pinewood already blackened the shadows of dusk. It was hard for her to see—yet she was certain she had caught sight of something moving in the trees, somewhere between the stage and her lookout.

Probably just an animal, she thought, telling herself that she was just getting jittery because of her upcoming performance. Just a squirrel . . . or maybe a raccoon. She tried to turn her attention back to the juggler who was keeping three oranges and two apples circling in the air. But for some reason she remained troubled.

And then . . . it happened again! This time, she was certain she saw something—a flash of white, a quick movement inside the protective shield of fat oak trees, something that just did not belong. She heard something, too—a footstep, or perhaps the crack of a branch breaking. Whatever it was, Chris felt chills run down her spine.

Her first instinct was to stay glued to the window. To keep watching until she discovered what it was she had seen and heard. But onstage, Sam was announcing Linda Ames and her Amazing Marionettes, the second-to-last act of the show. That meant that she was on next, that it was time for her to steal through the woods to take her place backstage.

Chris had no choice but to run through the darkness, through the patch of woods where she had just seen that undefinable, but nevertheless peculiar, movement. Where something was lurking . . . watching . . . waiting.

She shivered, then told herself that she was just being silly. But as she sprinted through the woods, she kept her eyes straight ahead, on the bright lights of the stage that was a few hundred feet ahead of her. It was as if not looking around too much would keep her from seeing anything she didn't really want to see.

By the time she reached the backstage area, her heart was pounding and her cheeks were flushed bright red. It was deserted except for Susan, Richard, and Sam, since the other counselors had joined the audience after completing their performances.

"Chris, what's wrong?" Susan demanded the instant she laid eyes on her twin. She grabbed her by the shoulders.

"You look as if you just saw a ghost!" Richard added. "You didn't . . . did you?"

"I'm not sure *what* I saw. In fact, I'm not even sure if I saw anything at all!"

Quickly, Chris related what had happened. Now that she was with the others, however, the whole thing sounded a bit foolish. After she finished, she added lamely, "But now I have a feeling I just imagined it all. Probably just some weird manifestation of stage fright. After all, I spent a long time just standing there in the dark, all alone, waiting to go on. That could make anybody see things!"

Susan and Richard pretended to agree. But all three of them suspected that Chris really *had* seen something. As for what that something was . . . well, this was hardly the time to wonder about it.

Sam was already introducing their act in her enthusiastic mistress of ceremonies voice.

"And now, for our final act of the evening. Here's something we're sure will impress and entertain you—even those of you who insist that you don't *really* believe in magic! The counselors' variety show is pleased to present . . . the Great Ricardo!"

"Break a leg!" Chris whispered hoarsely. Then she climbed into the false bottom of one of the two huge wooden packing crates on wheels that were among the props the three of them had spent the week building.

Richard and Susan paraded on stage, amid a burst of wild applause and cheers. Behind them they towed the two crates.

Accompanied by a recording of eerie-sounding music with an energetic beat, Richard opened the crates, one at a time, to show the attentive audience that they were empty. Chris, crouched in the bottom of one of them, listened carefully for her cue. She could tell that Susan had just gotten into the other one. She heard Richard slam them both shut, then hammer a few nails into each with a great flourish.

"Hokus-pokus, Pinewood-okus!" Richard bellowed, passing his magic wand over both crates. Hastily Chris punched out the thin "ceiling" that had kept her out of view, and struck a relaxed pose. By the time Richard pried open her crate, she was lounging in the middle of it, grinning as if she hadn't a care in the world.

The campers were astounded. She heard some of them actually gasp in surprise. It was a great feeling, being part of an act like this, one that the kids were finding so enthralling.

Chris climbed out of the crate and helped Richard push the two crates together. It was time for him to "saw her in half." When she got back in, it was her head and arms that stuck out of the hole on the side—but it was Susan's feet that extended out the other end.

Richard went on to do a few more tricks, those that didn't involve the twins. Chris was playing the role of assistant, while poor Susan remained tucked away in one of the crates.

She's going to be stiff tomorrow! Chris thought ruefully. But she kept a big smile plastered on her face—as any stage performer would, she reasoned.

By the time the Great Ricardo performed his final trick—putting his assistant behind a curtain, then making her disappear, only to reappear at the back of the theater—the campers were spellbound. They cheered and yelled so loudly as Richard and Susan took their final bows that they could no doubt be heard all the way across Lake Majestic. The magician and his assistant wore huge smiles of triumph as they stood onstage amidst an enthusiastic response.

Meanwhile, Chris was backstage, enjoying their act's success from the sidelines. She knew that she, too, should be lost in the excitement of the moment. But something was nagging at her. . . . Oh, yes. The mysterious "happening" of fifteen minutes or so earlier. It was still troubling her. And she knew that it would continue to trouble her until she found out what was behind it.

If anything, she reminded herself. It's possible that you really *did* imagine the whole thing.

For the moment, however, she was determined to

put it out of her mind. Susan and Richard were gleeful over the success of the evening's performance, and she didn't want to spoil their fun.

"You two were terrific!" said Chris as they joined her backstage.

"You were, too, Chris!"

"Susan's right; we couldn't have done it without you!" Richard grinned. "Now, how about us going over to the dining hall for some punch and cake, or whatever the Reeds have got lined up for us? I don't know about you, but I'm parched! Being a star is a lot of work!"

"Can't wait," said Chris. "Let me just change my clothes and get my story straight about how I was just released from the infirmary minutes ago. I'll meet you there as soon as I can."

One thing's for sure, she thought as she watched Susan and Richard join the throngs of counselors and campers who were slowly making their way toward the dining hall, chattering away excitedly about the performance they'd just seen. I'm going to get changed and join the others as fast as I can. After tonight, I have no intention of wandering around Camp Pinewood alone at night! Not as long as I keep seeing things!

Certain she was breaking the world's speed record for changing clothes, Chris pulled off her costume and climbed into a pair of jeans and a T-shirt.

Nine

As she hurried into the dining hall, dressed in her jeans and all her makeup scrubbed off, Chris saw that Susan and Richard were already enjoying "star treatment." Campers crowded around them as if they were celebrities. There was real electricity in the air as the kids begged to know more about the act—especially how they had managed to carry off all those impressive tricks. The magic act had easily been the hit of the entire show.

"But how did you *do* it?" little Lucy Kramer was demanding in her wheedling tone. "I never took my eyes off the stage, and I still don't know how you got from one crate to the other!"

"Maybe that really *is* a magic wand!" said Maggie, her eyes big and round with wonderment. "Is it, Richard?"

"Professional secret!" With a wink, Richard draped his arm around Susan's shoulders. "Neither

I nor my assistant and co-conspirator here will ever tell."

Just then, he noticed that Chris had come in. "Hey, look who's here! It's Chris! Feeling better?" he asked loudly.

"A lot better," Chris replied in the same loud voice. "All I needed was a day's rest in the infirmary. I'm almost as good as new."

"Oooh, too bad you had to miss the show!" said Maggie with surprising sympathy.

"Yes, too bad," Chris agreed, looking as disappointed as she could. "So how was it, anyway?"

A dozen campers crowded around her, anxious to describe in the greatest detail all the acts they had just seen onstage.

By the time she managed to break away from them, explaining that she still wasn't quite herself yet, Chris really did need a cold drink. She headed for the punch bowl, noticing that a huge cake had been cut up into slices on the next table. That, she decided, would be her next stop.

But as she stood in front of the giant punch bowl, she suddenly grew aware that someone was standing very close to her.

"Feeling better, Chris?"

It was Alan, she was pleased to see. "I'm fine now. Guess I just needed a rest." She wished she could tell him the truth. "How about you, though?" Her voice suddenly softened. "I understand something went wrong with those chairs you rented."

"Yeah. Another 'mystery,' I'm afraid. A whole shedful of chairs: now you see them, now you don't. More hokus-pokus than I saw in your sister's magic act."

"Oh, so you caught our act!" interrupted Richard, having heard only the end of their conversation. "What did you think? Are we ready for Broadway? Las Vegas? Hollywood?"

"Actually, I was pretty impressed," Alan admitted. "One of these days you'll have to explain to me how you managed to do those tricks."

"I think I have an idea," said Chris teasingly. "And I promise to tell you all about it the very first chance I get."

When the punchbowl was empty and even the most gung-ho of campers was getting drowsy, the party was pronounced over. Reluctant to have the evening end, the twins prepared to head back to their cabin.

"Hey, you're not going to sleep already, are you?" asked Richard.

"Sorry, but the glittering lights have taken their toll," Susan said with a laugh. "I'm wiped out. Even my creaky old cot is beginning to sound inviting."

Alan took Chris's hand. "Well, at least let us walk you home."

"Good idea," Richard agreed. "Then I can use my magic wand to scare away the ghosts you saw before, Chris."

"What ghosts?" Suddenly, Alan was very serious.

"Oh, it was nothing. At least, I *think* it was nothing. I was, um, a few hundred feet away from everybody else earlier tonight, during the show—actually, right by the arts and crafts building. And, well . . . I know it sounds silly now, but . . ."

"It doesn't sound silly at all. What did you see, Chris?"

"Well . . . I'm not really sure. Just some kind of movement. Something white, moving behind the trees. And I heard something, too. A footstep or a branch breaking . . . really, it could have been anything."

"It probably was nothing," Alan said uneasily. "Just the same, I think I'll mention it to my folks, if you don't mind."

The foursome headed up the path, toward Cabin Four. Dozens of others were also streaming uphill, joking and laughing as they went back to their cabins after an exhilarating evening. Still, they were among the last to straggle home. Behind them was nothing but silence and the blackness of night.

Suddenly, Richard stopped. He gripped Susan's arm tightly. "Wait a second. What was that?"

"I didn't hear anything." Nervously, Susan looked around. "What did it sound like?"

"I'm not sure . . . maybe it was nothing. It's just that all of a sudden I had this creepy feeling that we were being followed."

"Wish I'd brought along a flashlight," Chris muttered. She was aware of how dark it was in the woods, especially since the lights of the dining hall, far behind them, had just been turned off. And the four of them must have been walking slowly, because everyone else seemed to have moved on way ahead.

They were totally alone.

"I heard it again!" This time Richard's voice was a whisper. They all stood frozen, listening, unable to move. "Do you think we're being followed?"

"Naw, that's ridiculous." But the expression on Alan's face, totally drained of blood, said that he didn't really think it was ridiculous at all.

They stood still for a full minute—but heard nothing. It was Chris who finally broke the silence.

"Listen, I think that instead of running away, we should go after whoever's following us. Or whoever's hiding in the woods."

"You mean *now*?" Richard gulped. "In the dark?"

His fearfulness made her even braver. "For heaven's sake! How on earth will we ever get to the bottom of this if we don't take the bull by the horns and go *after* whoever it is who's doing all these things to Camp Pinewood?"

"Chris is right," Susan agreed. "We can't just run away."

"Okay," said Alan. "If that's how everybody feels, why don't we break up into two couples and take a quick look around? This area isn't that big. If there really is somebody hiding in the woods right now, we should have no trouble finding him."

Richard was all ready to ask, But what do we *do* if we find him? when the four of them heard a loud noise that made them all jump.

"Somebody just slammed a car door," said Alan. "Whoever was here is now on his way out."

"Let's follow him!" cried Chris. "Quick, where's the pickup truck?"

Alan led the way. The others followed him, hanging on to one another to keep from tripping over a stone or the root of a tree in the unfamiliar darkness. They scrambled into the truck—Alan and Chris in the cab, Susan and Richard in back.

"Leave the lights off," Chris warned as Alan turned the key in the ignition. For once, the battered old truck started right up. "That way, they won't realize they're being followed."

"Hey, you're pretty clever, you know that?"

Chris laughed nervously. "I've seen a lot of detective stories in the movies. Plus I've read every Nancy Drew mystery ever written!"

Alan's pickup hurried along the dirt road for a few hundred feet. He had an advantage over anyone else driving that road; every square inch, every dip and pothole, was familiar to him. Even with only the light of the moon and the stars to help him see, he managed to maneuver his truck quickly and with ease. Before long, they spotted a car up ahead.

"There he is!" Chris whispered hoarsely. "He's turning right, onto the main road. Let's follow him! But stay back, so he can't see us."

"I'll have to turn on the headlights. . . ."

"I know. But hopefully he'll think we're just another car, traveling this road behind him."

Alan drove slowly, staying a few car lengths behind. The other car neither speeded up nor slowed down—a good sign, Chris concluded. He didn't seem to suspect that he was being followed.

Then he signaled a right turn and eased off the road. Chris leaned forward in her seat, peering through the windshield.

"What's that? Where is he stopping?"

Alan groaned—then laughed. "We're out of luck, I'm afraid. That happens to be the Okie-Dokie Inn, our neighborhood tavern. Unless you're willing to go inside, I'm afraid this is where our chase has to end."

Sure enough, as they drove by, Chris saw that it was indeed a restaurant and bar. And given the dozen or so cars parked in front, it was impossible to tell which car was the one they'd been following.

"Dead end," she sighed. "Might as well turn around and go home."

As Alan drove into the parking lot, Chris took a closer look at the Okie-Dokie Inn. It was a seedy-looking establishment, really a small white-shingled house with peeling brown shutters that had been converted into a tavern. A red neon sign advertising one particular brand of beer blinked on and off in its main window. There was something sad about that little roadside inn, Chris thought.

But as Alan put the truck in reverse, preparing to back out of the parking lot once again, his head-lights passed over another building, right behind the Okie-Dokie. It shared the same parking lot—yet she hadn't noticed it before. It was long and flat, with several separate entrances, like a motel. They reminded her of doctors' offices, or one of those buildings that housed small businesses. What was most interesting, however, was the fact that for one brief second, Alan's lights illuminated what looked like a man.

A man wearing who was wearing a white shirt.

Chris glanced at Alan, wanting to see if he, too, noticed the man headed toward one of the doorways in the office building. But he seemed intent on studying the rear-view mirror as he backed out, onto the main road.

Something stopped Chris from saying anything to him. Instead, she decided to keep her observation to herself—at least for now.

And then, all of a sudden, he said, "I'm kind of glad we lost that guy, Chris. We don't know who he was or what he wanted. . . . He could even be dangerous. I know we all got caught up in the moment back there, but from now on I think we should leave the sleuthing to people who know what they're doing. I'll tell my parents we spotted a trespasser and that we followed him here. Maybe they'll just let it pass . . . or maybe they'll call in the police. But this kind of thing is definitely out of my league."

Chris knew then that she had made the right decision. Alan was probably right; he wasn't the one to do the "sleuthing." No, it was something that should be left to the experts. To the masterminds. Those clever people who could put their heads together and outsmart the bad guys.

She made a firm resolution then. She and Susan would get started on it first thing the very next day.

Ten

Later that night, when all the lights around camp were out and Sam and Linda's even breathing indicated that they were both sound asleep, Chris called a powwow with her twin.

"Sooz, we have to talk," she announced, careful to keep her voice low enough that their cabinmates wouldn't wake up.

"I had a feeling you'd suggest that sooner or later."

The two girls were lying in their cots, pushed together so that they could talk softly and still hear each other. Outside the cabin, the night was black and silent, broken only by the occasional glimmer of a firefly and the rhythmic chirping of crickets.

"What did you think of our little 'chase' tonight?"

Susan thought only for a second. "First of all, I think the man we caught lurking in the woods and then making a quick getaway in his car probably had something to do with the disappearing chairs. And possibly some—or all—of the other things that have gone on around here during the last few summers."

"I agree," Chris interjected. "I mean, I don't think he was just somebody who happened to wander into Camp Pinewood for the evening. For one thing, he seemed to know his way around a little too well."

"Right. Besides, he must have hidden his car behind some trees or something. Otherwise, Mr. Reed or Alan or somebody would have realized sooner that he was hanging around."

"Good point. What else?"

"Second, I noticed that there's more to the Okie-Dokie Inn than meets the eye. Mainly, some kind of office building, right behind it. I have a feeling that the phantom we were chasing tonight could well have ended up in one of those offices."

Chris's face lit up. "Sooz, I can't believe you said that! You know, as Alan was turning the car around in the parking lot, I saw a man walking toward one of the doorways! And he was wearing a white shirt!"

"A white shirt—just like the 'ghost' you saw before, during the counselors' variety show!" Susan was growing so excited that she was ready to bounce right out of bed. "Well, then, there's only one thing for us to do. Tomorrow, one of us has to go back there and investigate."

"Exactly what I was thinking. Our first step is to find out who has offices back there. . . ."

"And what kind of business they're engaged in."

Chris thought for a minute. "How are we going to get there? I didn't really notice how far away it was. It was hard, in the dark. . . ."

"Walking distance, I'm sure. After all, we were only on the main road for two or three minutes. And Alan was driving pretty slowly."

"That's true. Now all we need is a way for one of us to sneak away."

"That could be tough." Susan was pensive for a moment. "You and I both have classes to teach in the morning. You have Beginners' Swimming at nine, right? And I have an arts and crafts group at ten. Do you think an hour is enough time to get over to the Okie-Dokie and do some snooping around?"

"Maybe . . . maybe not. But I have a better idea."

Even in the pale light of the moon, Susan saw in her twin's brown eyes a mischievous gleam that she recognized only too well. "Uh, oh. What have you got up your sleeve, Christine Pratt?"

"Only a harmless little scheme."

"I'm afraid to ask. . . ."

"Listen. How about if right after breakfast I sneak away to the Okie-Dokie to see what I can find out. You, meanwhile, pretend to be me from nine until ten, and teach my swimming class. And then, at ten, you can go on to teach arts and crafts. That way, I'll have plenty of time."

"Great—except for one small problem."

"What's that?" Chris could see no flaws in her plan.

"Chris, how can I teach swimming to a bunch of little kids? I'm not qualified to do that!"

"Can't you come up with some clever solution?"

When she saw the look of dismay on Susan's face, she added, "After all, you always have in the past. You've pretended to be me before, and you always came up with ways of getting around these sticky situations."

"'Sticky situations'? You call twenty little kids who can't swim splashing around a lake a 'sticky situation'?"

"Come on, Sooz. Where's the old Pratt ingenuity? Don't tell me you can't come up with *something*. Why, I'd be disappointed in you if you couldn't!"

Susan cast her twin a rueful glance. "Well, if you really think that's the best way to go about this, I suppose I can think up a way to entertain a bunch of eight-year-olds that enables them to keep their noses above water. I'll sleep on it."

"Great. See, I knew you could do it! Now, here's what we'll do. I'll sneak away right after breakfast, while everybody's still in the dining hall. You dress in something neutral, something either of us would wear. . . ."

"How about jeans and a Camp Pinewood T-shirt?"

"Perfect. I'll meet you here at the cabin at eleven o'clock, no matter what. Two hours . . . that should give me enough time to find out *something*."

The two girls were silent then, each one lost in her own thoughts, gradually drifting off to sleep. Just as Chris was about to doze off, she heard Susan say, "Hey, Chris?" in a barely audible voice.

"Yes, Sooz." She was surprised her sister was still awake.

"Promise me one thing, okay?"

"Sure. What?"

"The next time there's some investigating to be done on this thing, it'll be my turn to go sleuthing. To help out. Okay? I mean, I don't want you to end up doing all the work yourself. After all, I want to do something to help the Reeds, too."

Chris chuckled softly. "Sure, Sooz. That's only fair, right?"

Both girls drifted off to sleep, satisfied that they were doing something to help.

The fact that they might be getting in over their heads never even occurred to them.

The next morning, Susan awoke with a feeling of dread—mingled with gleeful anticipation. Then she remembered. Today she was going to pretend to be Chris. But only for an hour. She would have to switch gears quickly, becoming Susan again without missing a beat.

Over breakfast, she and Chris were quiet. They had dressed the same, wanting everyone at camp to see that for a change they looked identical. In fact, several campers and counselors commented on how unusual it was for them to be wearing the same clothes.

"Just a coincidence," they replied with a smile, glad they had chosen such simple outfits, something that they both might wear and feel comfortable in.

Immediately after breakfast, Chris slipped away, back to the cabin to change into one of the sundresses she'd brought, an outfit that wouldn't identify her at all with Camp Pinewood. And Susan headed for the lake, a bit apprehensive about her very first attempt at teaching swimming. Or, more accurately, at *not* teaching swimming, since she had no intention of leading a group of eight-year-olds into the lake, trying to keep an eye on all twenty of them at once.

The campers were already waiting for her, wearing their bathing suits and clutching their towels. Fortunately, Chris had reminded her to put on *her* bathing suit, underneath her jeans and T-shirt. She was so nervous that she might have forgotten otherwise.

"Hey, Chris, how come you're not wearing your bathing suit today?" asked one little girl, with freckles and red hair braided into two pigtails.

In response, Susan pulled off her T-shirt to reveal one of Chris's kelly-green tank suits.

"You never did *that* before." The little girl looked troubled. "Aren't we going into the water today?"

"As a matter of fact, I came up with an idea for something different for us to do this morning."

The campers looked doubtful. Obviously, most of them considered their morning dip in the lake one of the high points of the day. She realized that her plan to discuss water safety—while on dry land—was not going to go over as well as she'd hoped.

Susan could feel herself floundering. How was she going to keep these water babies entertained for an hour? Having them stay right next to Lake Majestic yet not letting them go in seemed like a sort of punishment.

"*I* know!" She was suddenly inspired. "What we're going to do today is take turns giving a swimming exhibition. One at a time, I'd like you to jump into the water and then show the rest of us how well you can swim. You know, what you've learned so far this year. Everyone else will be sitting on the dock, watching. They'll be your audience. It's like putting on a show, in a way."

While she felt uneasy about keeping an eye on twenty kids in the water, she could certainly deal with one at a time. Even *her* lifeguarding skills were strong enough for that.

"So, what do you think, kids?"

"Yippeee!" cried the little girl with the braids. "Just like the counselors' variety show last night! We can all take turns being the *star*!"

"Oh, boy! I can show everyone how well I can float!" chirped another.

"And *I* can show everyone how well I can *dive*! My brother taught me how, last summer!"

The campers buzzed happily as they thought up ways to show off their newly acquired swimming skills and tried to come up with special effects to embellish their "acts."

Relieved, Susan thanked her lucky stars that she was fairly good at thinking on her feet.

She only hoped her twin sister, no doubt already poking around behind the Okie-Dokie Inn, was doing half as well.

Eleven

The walk from Camp Pinewood to the Okie-Dokie Inn was longer than Chris remembered it being. The night before, as the pickup cruised along the main road, it seemed as if it were only a mile or so away. But as she trudged along that morning, the sun growing hotter and hotter with each step, she found herself wondering how she could have miscalculated by so much.

She was also worried about whether her twin would be able to hold down the fort all morning.

That's the *least* of your worries, she told herself firmly as she tromped along the shoulder of the road, watching her beige leather sandals and her toes becoming coated with a thin film of dust. Sooz will be fine. She always was before.

No, it was not Susan's mission that she should be concerned about, she knew. It was her *own* mission.

Now that she was headed for the Okie-Dokie,

dressed in a lavender sundress that she hoped would make her look like just another one of the locals, rather than a representative of Camp Pinewood, it occurred to her that she still wasn't sure of what she intended to do once she got there. She mainly planned to investigate that long flat building behind the tavern, the one both twins had noticed last night. *And* the place where she was certain she'd seen a man in a white shirt walking.

But as she continued her hike, she had to admit that she was already less enthusiastic than she'd been the night before. She was afraid that she would learn very little. That what was supposed to be the first step in her "sleuthing" would turn out to be nothing more than a dead end.

Finally, after crossing over a grassy patch at a bend in the road, the Inn came into view. She was relieved that she had finally reached her destination—but at the same time, the butterflies in her stomach reminded her how nervous she was about this little expedition.

In the morning light, the Okie-Dokie Inn looked even more dilapidated than it had the night before. Its roof sagged slightly, its white shingles badly needed painting, and its small windows, now dark, reminded Chris of blank, staring eyes.

But it wasn't the Okie-Dokie itself that she was interested in. It was the office building behind it, half-hidden by the tavern. As Chris neared it, she instinctively moved slowly, being careful to stay in the shadows. She found a lookout at the side of the Inn, between the back "porch" and a huge green metal dumpster. Fortunately, no one was around.

The Inn was all closed up, as she suspected it would be for a few hours yet.

From her carefully chosen hideout, Chris had a good view of the offices and the parking lot. There were already several cars parked there, but no one was around. She decided that walking by each doorway would be safe enough, since there was nobody there even to notice her, much less to wonder what she was doing there. She stood up straight, clutched at her shoulder bag, and confidently strode out from the shadows, toward the walkway that ran the length of the building.

The first door was plainly marked with two placards: "Dr. Silver, D.D.S." and "Dr. Morgan, D.D.S." Two dentists' offices. Chris frowned, then walked by. Unless Camp Pinewood's prowler was a dentist, chances were slim that this was the place to which he had retreated last night. Besides, she was certain that the man who had been illuminated by the headlights of Alan's pickup truck had been heading down the other way.

The second door had a bigger sign. "Taylor Temps," it read. "Temporary Typing Services. By the Hour, By the Day."

There, that was a relief. If anyone happened to ask her what she was doing, lurking about, she could always say she was looking for Taylor Temps. To find out about a job. A *summer* job. She smiled to herself over the fact that she would, in a way, be telling the truth.

That offered her an alibi—but it didn't help her investigation any. She was beginning to get discouraged. Maybe walking over here like this, just to read the names on the doors, was nothing more than a waste of time. Still, she was determined to continue. She had come this far, and she wasn't about to turn back now.

Doorways three and four offered little of interest, Chris was chagrined to discover. One was an accountant's office; the other, a lawyer's. Again, she wondered if either of them belonged to the mystery man. But even if one did, there was little she could learn by loitering outside their entrances.

She was surprised to see that there was a fifth doorway, tucked away at the very end of the building. She hadn't noticed it before. That could well have been where the man was headed last night. . . . She crossed her fingers.

Before she could reach the door, Chris had to pass by a large window, one that no doubt opened onto the front office or waiting room. She hoped that anyone in there would be too busy to notice her—especially since she fully intended to peer inside to see whatever she could see.

She strode by assuredly—but not too quickly. Her eyes were glued to the room inside, as if she expected to find there exactly what she was looking for—whatever *that* was. So she couldn't help being disappointed when all she saw was a receptionist, behind a desk, talking on the telephone.

Well, what did you expect? she thought.

She was about to give up and go back to Camp Pinewood when she noticed the sign on the door down at the end of the building. It read, "Lake Majestic Realty Company."

Suddenly, something clicked inside her head.

Realty . . . real estate . . . property . . . land. A company whose business was buying and selling land. Near Lake Majestic. Large pieces of land, perhaps . . . like that occupied by Camp Pinewood. And this establishment was in the same direction the man she spotted the night before had been headed.

It was a longshot, she knew. But still, she had a hunch she had found the right place.

Chris's heart was pounding. If this *was* the right place, what should she do? She couldn't very well barge in and demand to know what was going on. Ask them why they were so interested in Camp Pinewood. Why their employees were prowling around its grounds at night. And perhaps even why they were bothering to play little tricks—like stealing chairs or hiding cartons of supplies or letting all the boats drift out onto the lake. No, being so direct would get her nowhere.

But then . . . what *should* she do? Chris retreated to the side of the building, out of sight of the line of windows and doors that faced the main road. She needed a minute to think, to decide what she should do. She wondered if it was getting late. The sun seemed to be getting so much higher in the sky, yet she couldn't have been away from camp for *that* long.

It was cool at the side of the building, as that section was cast in shadow. She leaned against the cool brick wall, glad for the chance to rest, to get out of the hot sun, if only for a few seconds. But her mind was racing.

If only Susan were here! she thought mournfully. She always came up with good ideas. Maybe she could telephone her, tell her what she'd discovered, explain what her hunch was. . . .

And then Chris became aware of something she hadn't noticed before: the soft buzz of voices. The sound was coming from the back of the building, she realized. Stealthily she crept along the wall, until she came to the corner. Sure enough, the back of the building was lined with small windows, one for each of the five offices. And they were all high enough so that anyone could stand underneath, without being seen . . . and listen.

Chris followed the sound of the voices, growing more and more excited. Sure enough, they were coming from the back office of the Lake Majestic Realty Company. The window was wide open, and the people who were speaking seemed to be standing or sitting right in front of it.

"I think we finally managed to do it!" a male voice was saying, loudly and triumphantly. "You should have seen the looks on those kids' faces when they found out their evening was ruined! Hiding all those chairs in the woods was a real brainstorm, Tom!"

"Yeah, well, the kids' reactions don't matter one bit," another man replied, his tone sour. "What we need is for their *parents* to get mad."

"Well, I'm sure they will. If what happened last night doesn't do it, just wait until you see the little scheme I planned for this morning! I think I've really outdone myself this time! The parents will be dragging their kids out of Camp Pinewood so fast that the little darlings won't even know what hit 'em!"

"Good work, Pete. Hopefully, all this will mean lots of complaints, irate parents demanding their money back . . . and financial problems for the

Reeds. The slow but sure demise of Camp Pinewood. Otherwise, we'll never be able to get that
land away from them."

"Not for a price we can afford, anyway," agreed
the first man, Pete.

His associate laughed wickedly. "Oh, we could
afford it, Pete. It's simply that we don't want to
have to *pay* it! Not if we can get that land away
from them for peanuts."

"Right, Tom! By next week, we'll have the
Reeds thinking we're doing them a favor by taking
that property off their hands. In fact, I can hardly
wait to see the looks of gratitude on their faces at
the public land auction next Wednesday!"

Chris was dumbfounded. So *that* was what was
going on! These evil men had been sabotaging
Camp Pinewood so they could force the Reeds
out—and buy their land at a low, and unfair, price!
She stayed very still, anxious to hear more. She
only hoped that her pounding heart wouldn't give
her away.

"Ahhh, just wait until you see the condominiums
we're going to build on that spot, Pete!" the second
man, Tom, was saying. "You and I will be
millionaires by next summer. How many apart-
ments do you think we can crowd onto those few
acres, anyway? And don't forget: the more we can
fit, the richer we'll be!"

Just then a door opened. The clacking sound of
high heels told Chris that a third person—a woman—had just come into the room.

"Good news, gentlemen!" she said jubilantly. "I
just talked to Betty, over at Town Hall. Jake Reed
called the Office of Land and Zoning this morning,

just a few minutes ago. He's putting Camp Pine-wood up for public auction next week!''

Oh, no! Chris groaned to herself, even as she heard Tom and Pete and the woman congratulating one another and laughing over their success. I just hope it's not too late. . . .

"All right, now. Everybody back to work. Pete, Doris, we've all got things to do before next Wednesday's land auction.'' That was Tom, who was apparently the boss. "I, for one, am going to start calling some architects. The planning of Waterfront Condominiums, the real estate devel-opment project that's going to make us all rich, has now officially begun!''

It was all Chris could do to keep from running back to Camp Pinewood. She was still afraid of being seen, though—by Tom or Pete or anyone else who worked at the Lake Majestic Realty Company. They *were* dangerous people; Alan had been right. But he had had no idea of *how* dangerous they were—or in what ways.

She smoothed her dress, patted her hair, and walked away from the office building, trying to look calm. It wasn't until she was on the main road that she broke into a jog. She was anxious to get back, to talk to her sister, to figure out what steps to take.

She was relieved that she had finally found out what was going on at Camp Pinewood.

Now, if only there were something she and Susan could *do* about it!

Twelve

As soon as Chris hurried into the center of camp, after stopping off at her cabin for a quick change of clothes, she knew that something had gone wrong. There was a great deal of commotion over at the arts and crafts building. The whole camp, it seemed, had gathered there—and it was obvious that it was hardly for a happy occasion.

She spotted Alan, standing at the edge of the crowd.

"What happened?"

He glanced at her sadly. "Somebody got into the arts and crafts building sometime between last night and this morning and destroyed all the kids' art projects from the whole summer."

"Oh, no!" Chris began to feel dizzy.

"Smashed up their paper hats, their papier-mâché sculptures, their drawings . . . everything."

"Oh, Alan! I'm so sorry!"

"Yeah, me too," he replied with a cold smile. "There goes our annual art exhibition, during Parents' Day, at the end of next week." He shook his head slowly. "Once again, Camp Pinewood comes out looking like some two-bit operation."

Just like that man said, thought Chris, so angry that she was close to tears. That . . . that *Pete* had said he'd done something else this morning. Something that would make the campers—and their parents—very mad indeed.

"Where's Susan? I'd better go find her." Suddenly, Chris's concern was for her sister. She spotted her in front of the building, standing with a group of ten-year-olds, her ten o'clock class. And, she could tell by their faces, they were even more distraught over the senseless—and unexplained—destruction than anyone.

Lucy Kramer, true to form, was already up in arms. And her pouting was aggravating what was already a shaky situation. All the campers were upset, and the last thing they needed was to listen to her whining.

"I just called my parents!" Lucy was announcing loudly. "I told them all about this horrible, stupid camp. And I told them how much I hate it here now. Boy, we won't even be able to show off our art projects on Parents' Day next week! And I spent *hours* working on my pipe cleaner zoo!"

"I'm sure you'll get over it, Lucy." Susan tried consoling her. But this time her attempts at calming the little girl down were falling on deaf ears.

"Well, they're on their way to pick me up, right now. They're going to take me away from this crummy old place! And I bet they're going to want to get all their money back, besides!"

She turned to her sidekick, Maggie. "And you're going to call *your* parents, too. Right, Maggie? To have them come take you away from this awful camp?"

"I-I guess so," Maggie agreed meekly.

Susan looked relieved when she spotted her twin, headed toward her.

"Chris! *There* you are! I was wondering what was taking you so long!"

Chris cast her a meaningful look. "Well, it turned out to be worth it. Especially given this latest development." She looked around sadly.

"Really? You mean you found out something?"

"I sure did. But now that I've done my part, I need you for advice. Maybe you can figure out what you and I should do next. But first, let's go somewhere where no one can hear us."

The two girls snuck away to their cabin. Fortunately, Linda and Sam were still at the arts and crafts building, trying to maintain order among the disappointed campers.

Chris sat down on her bed and proceeded to tell her sister about the conversation she had overheard while lurking underneath the back window of the Lake Majestic Realty Company's offices. Susan, sitting at the foot, listened to every word. Her brown eyes grew big and round as the meaning of what her sister was saying began to sink in. By the time her sister had finished, she was ready to burst.

"Chris, we've got to *do* something! We can't let those . . . those *criminals* get away with this!"

"I know," Chris replied seriously. "But what can we do?"

Susan thought for a minute. "I suppose we should go right over and tell the Reeds what you found out today."

"That's what occurred to me, too. At least, at first. But now I'm not so sure."

Susan was surprised. "Why on earth *not*?"

"Because we have no real proof, that's why not." Chris leaned forward earnestly. "Look, if we tell Mr. and Mrs. Reed what you overheard, and they go to the police—or even to those Lake Majestic Realty people themselves—it becomes an issue of *my* word against *theirs*."

"That's true. All they have to do is deny it." Susan looked morose. "And considering the fact that they're probably one of the town's upstanding businesses and you're someone who doesn't even *live* around here, I suppose it's pretty safe to assume that your credibility in these parts would be pretty low."

"Exactly. So we're back to Square One. What we need here is some *proof* of what they've been doing." Suddenly, Chris flopped across the bed and groaned. "Great! How are we *ever* going to manage that? I feel like we've just hit a real dead end. Here we know precisely what's been going on, but we can't do a *thing* about it. . . ."

"Don't be so sure." Susan's voice was so soft that her twin hardly heard her.

"What? You mean you have an idea?" Excited once again, Chris sat up abruptly. "Oh, I knew you'd come up with something, Sooz. You're so good at this kind of thing! What have you got?"

"It's simple," she replied calmly. "One of us will just have to sneak inside and find some evidence."

"Evidence?"

"Yes. Like a letter or a memo . . . something in writing."

Chris flopped back down on the bed again. "Oh, Sooz! *That's* no good! In fact, it's *impossible!*" She thought for a moment. "It also happens to be illegal. Isn't that considered 'breaking and entering'?"

"I suppose it is, if you want to get technical about it. Still, it is for a good cause. . . ."

"Wait a minute. I think this is already getting way out of hand!"

Susan sighed. "You're right. It *is* a bit much. If only there were a way one of us could get into their offices legally, without actually picking their locks or climbing in through their windows. All we'd need is a few minutes to do some quick snooping around. . . ."

The two girls were silent for a minute or two, each one lost in her own thoughts. It certainly seemed as if what they wanted to do was impossible. . . .

And then, all of a sudden, Chris snapped her fingers.

"I've got it!" she cried triumphantly. "At least, I *think* I've got it!"

"Let's hear it. At this point, any suggestion is bound to sound like a good one."

"Okay, here goes." Chris's cheeks grew pink as she spoke. "While I was looking around those offices this morning, I noticed that one of them, just a few doors down from Lake Majestic Realty, is a temporary typing agency. It's called Taylor Temps, I think. They supply typists by the day or by the hour."

"So?"

"Well, you may recall that I took typing in school last year."

"So did I. Everyone does, sooner or later. It's required at Whittington High, in order to graduate. I still don't understand what that has to do with anything."

"I'll just pretend that I work for Taylor Temps! I'll show up at the Realty office at lunchtime and say that Tom or Pete or Doris hired me to fill in for the hour. Then I'll have access to all their files while everyone's out to lunch—including their receptionist!"

"Christine Pratt, I'm surprised at you. Would you actually have the nerve to do that?"

"Not unless we'd done some research first. I'd want to make sure everyone really *was* going to be out of the office, for one thing. . . ."

"And how do you propose we do that?"

Chris was quiet for a minute, but it was obvious that her mind was ticking away. "We'll just have to take turns casing the joint."

"'Casing the joint'!" Susan burst out laughing. "Now I *know* you've seen too many spy movies!"

"What I mean is, we'll just watch, from behind the Okie-Dokie Inn. We can find out what the normal office routine is, just by hanging around at lunchtime for a few days and watching everybody's comings and goings."

"That *does* sound simple. Even so, it could be risky. . . ."

"Of course it's risky!" Chris cried. She was beginning to get exasperated. "But we have to do *something*! We agreed on that ages ago! And I'm willing to take a few risks to help out the Reeds. Aren't you?"

"I guess so." Susan was surprised by her twin's earnestness. She was also moved by it. "Okay, I'm game. I suppose if anything goes wrong, we can always talk our way out of it. You and I both seem to be pretty good at that," she added with a grin.

"Oh, thanks, Sooz!" Chris leaned over and gave her twin a big hug. "I knew you'd come through."

For the next few days, Chris and Susan were busy. They took turns trekking over to the Okie-Dokie Inn around lunch time, while the twin who stayed at Camp Pinewood took on the other twin's responsibilities—and identity. It was a good thing they already had some experience in that area, as they repeatedly told each other, laughing about their ability to become each other—at least for a while.

And their surveillance of the Lake Majestic Realty Company's offices told them exactly what they needed to know. Every day, at around noon, two men and a woman left the office, sometimes together, sometimes separately, but always at about the same time. The twins figured out that they were the real estate agents, Tom and Pete and Doris, the three people Chris had overheard talking during her very first "visit." Then, about fifteen minutes later, the receptionist, whom Chris had also spotted that first day, left, locking the office door behind her. All four came back between one and one-thirty. That meant the office was completely empty between twelve-fifteen and one o'clock—a full forty-five minutes.

"There's something else I realized," Susan reported to Chris one afternoon, after returning from her shift. "The receptionist never goes out to lunch with anyone from the Taylor Temps office."

"That's good!" Chris understood immediately what she was driving at. "That way, when I tell her I'm a Taylor Temp, she won't find out over lunch with the Taylor Temps people that I'm a fraud!"

It wasn't until Wednesday, the day of the public land auction, that Chris felt she was ready to go ahead with the plan. It was just as well, she decided; if the real estate people *did* figure out that something funny was going on, they wouldn't have enough time to do anything about it. The auction was scheduled for two o'clock. That would give her just enough time to get her "proof" and hurry over to Town Hall. Susan, back at camp, would tell Alan everything at lunch, and he would drive over in his pickup truck, take her to Town Hall, and accompany her to the auction, where she would deliver the evidence—all in time to stop the Reeds from signing their land over to the Lake Majestic Realty Company. The plan sounded completely foolproof.

Even so, when Wednesday morning dawned, Chris was nervous. There were a lot of things that could go wrong . . . but she tried not to think about them. Instead, she tried to concentrate on the fact that she was doing what was best for Camp Pinewood—and the Reeds.

Now, if only I can carry it off successfully, she thought, glancing in the mirror one last time before sneaking away from Camp Pinewood, wanting to be certain she looked like an office worker and not a camp counselor. Acting was something that came to her easily, and she did have some experience, what with all the times she and Susan had traded places, pretending to be each other.

But as she headed for the Lake Majestic Realty Company's offices, there were butterflies in her stomach. This acting role was definitely the most challenging—*and* the most important—she had ever faced.

Thirteen

"Good afternoon!" Chris said heartily. "I hope I'm not late!"

She had just strode into the front office of the Lake Majestic Realty Company, where she was confronted by a very surprised-looking receptionist. It was the same woman she had been watching for the last few days, and she felt almost as if she knew her—even though she didn't even know her name.

The woman behind the desk looked at her blankly. "Can I help you with something?"

"Actually, I'm here to help *you*. I'm from Taylor Temps. You know, the temporary typing agency. . . ."

"Yes, I know the name. But I still don't understand why you're here. . . ."

"Oh." Chris pretended to be puzzled. "Well, gee, I was hired to fill in for the receptionist here during lunch hour today. I guess that's you, right?

Apparently your office is expecting some important phone calls, and they wanted to make sure someone was here to take them."

The receptionist frowned. "No one said anything to *me* about this."

"Really? Well, frankly, I don't know too much about it myself. Just that I was supposed to report to someone named Tom, at noon sharp."

"Oh, Tom. *That* figures." The receptionist sounded exasperated. "He never tells me *anything*. Just keeps piling on the work, without any regard to how much I have to do. . . ."

"Is Tom here?" Chris asked innocently.

"No, he left for lunch about five minutes ago. I'm afraid you just missed him."

"Oh, dear. That's too bad."

Of course, Chris knew only too well that Tom had just left, along with the other two real estate agents. After all, she had been standing in the shadows of the Okie-Dokie Inn, next to the dumpster, for a full fifteen minutes, waiting until the coast was clear.

"It doesn't matter, though." The receptionist shrugged. "In fact, now that you're here, I can take off a few minutes early." Conspiratorially, she added, "My lunch hour doesn't officially begin until twelve-fifteen. But if you're going to cover the phones, I might as well sneak out now. Hey, that means I'll even have time to go to the bank!"

"Take your time," said Chris breezily.

After a quick tour of the offices, during which Chris was able to identify Tom's office—and the office's key filing cabinet—and a brief lecture on how the telephone system worked, the receptionist hurried away. Her glee over getting out of the office a few minutes early kept her from asking a lot of questions—exactly what Chris had been hoping for.

Well, *that* was easy enough! she thought, greatly relieved once the woman was gone and she had the office to herself. Now, if only I can keep my hands from shaking. . . .

Chris got down to business immediately. She started with the file cabinet she had noticed first, right in Tom's office. It was very organized, with a separate file, it seemed, for each of their clients, all alphabetized. She checked under "R" for Reed and "P" for Pinewood, but found nothing. So she began reading through the files, one at a time, hoping to stumble upon something that rang a bell.

At first, she was nervous. Each noise made her jump. It hadn't occurred to her until she was actually doing this—going through Lake Majestic Realty's files, pretending to be someone she wasn't—how much of a risk she really was taking. What if someone came back early? She could be caught red-handed!

But that won't happen, she kept telling herself over and over again. Susan and I already checked all that out. The real estate agents never come back before one . . . so there's still plenty of time.

The other concern that plagued her was that what she was doing was probably illegal.

But what *they're* doing is illegal, too! she thought.

No, this was no time to be debating the pros and cons of what she was doing. She had already come this far. Now she had no choice but to go ahead with her plan. After all, it was all for the Reeds. And reminding herself of that made it much easier to continue.

As she became more and more involved with seeking out the information she so desperately needed, Chris forgot to be nervous. Instead, she found herself becoming angry.

Darn! I *know* there's something here! If only I could find it!

She gave up on the large filing cabinet. But another quick tour of the offices told her there weren't any other such files.

That left the desks.

Somehow, snooping around someone's desk seemed like a real violation of privacy. But once again she reminded herself that it was for a good cause. All she had to do was think about the conversation she had overheard—Tom's evil laugh, his plans to get rich in such an underhanded fashion, his triumph over forcing the Reeds to sell their land, and at too low a price. She forged onward, more determined than ever to expose the crooked dealings of Lake Majestic Reality. After taking a deep breath, she descended upon Tom's desk.

One drawer, she discovered, contained more files, like those she had found in the big file cabinet. Chris wondered why these were kept separately . . . unless they were *all* files on unethical dealings. She pounced upon them eagerly.

Sure enough, the third file she came across was labeled "Pinewood." And inside the manila envelope were six or eight memos and letters, all of them concerning the Reeds' property.

The memos were written to the real estate agents who worked in the office. Chris's eyes grew round as she skimmed them. They talked about plans for upsetting things at the camp—hiding supplies, releasing all the boats onto Lake Majestic, even hiding the folding chairs, rented for the counselors' show. And the tone of all of them was the same: congratulating Pete for successfully carrying out the evil little schemes that Tom had thought up.

At the back of the folder was a letter, written just a few days before. It was to a local architecture firm, describing the Reeds' property, which, the letter said, the Lake Majestic Realty Company "expected to acquire sometime in the near future." Tom suggested in the letter that the architects begin drawing up plans for a complex of lakefront condominiums. There was even a reference to the fact that saving money on the buildings, by "cutting corners wherever possible," was much more important than quality. Chris was astounded.

The folder was a gold mine! She had found exactly what she had come looking for. Now all she had to do was make a copy of each of the memos and the letter, get out while she still had the time, and hide behind the inn and wait for Alan and Susan to come by and pick her up. Once she presented copies of these documents at the public land auction, everyone would know exactly what had been going on. The game would be over for the Lake Majestic Realty Company!

But she had to hurry. The clock on Tom's desk told her it was ten minutes to one. She rushed over to the copying machine in the front room and quickly made two duplicates of each piece of paper. As she did she heard a car door slam—and jumped about two feet.

It could be anyone, she told herself. It's still early. That's probably just someone on his way to the dentist. You've still got time. . . .

With the copies in one hand and the originals in the other, Chris rushed back to Tom's office. She pulled open his desk drawer and leaned over to put the entire folder back exactly as she had found it. She was struggling to fit it in between two other folders when a sinking feeling suddenly traveled over her, making her break out in a cold sweat.

She knew even before she looked up that someone was standing in the doorway.

"Looks to me like I've got myself a burglar," growled the large, heavyset man who was looming before her.

Chris immediately recognized his voice as Tom's. Her knees felt so weak that she was certain she would sink to the floor. But instead, she just froze.

"But you're not just any old burglar. You've been going through my files, haven't you?"

Chris just stared at him. She had, indeed, been caught red-handed. She had his file in one hand, her copies of its contents in the other. What she had been doing was all too obvious—especially to someone like Tom, who knew that he was on the verge of completing the shady deal he'd started two or three years before.

When he walked over and calmly took both the folder and the copies away from her, Chris recoiled. And as he glanced at them, she told herself to run while she still could. Her legs didn't want to move, at first. It was like a nightmare, where she knew she had to get away but was frozen to the spot. And then, when she finally did manage to start hurrying away, he grabbed her roughly by the arm.

"Not so fast, honey. You think you're just going to walk right out of here? Especially since it's all too clear what you've been up to! No, you're a real troublemaker. Sent over by Jake Reed, I suppose. . . ."

"No! He doesn't know anything about this! And if you let me go, I promise not to say anything. . . ."

"'You promise'!" Tom laughed coldly. "And you think I should believe you, huh? Well, I'll let you go—in due time. But for the next couple of hours, I think it'd be best if I made sure a little troublemaker like you stayed out of the way!"

With that, he pushed her into a small storage room with no window, just an air vent, throwing in the folder and all the papers after her. "Here, that'll give you something to read while you're in there! Don't worry; you'll get out soon enough. Just as soon as the land auction is over! And by the way, if you should get any ideas about pounding on the door and yelling your head off, I'll be leaving a note on the door, telling Nancy to take the afternoon off.

"Now I've got a meeting to get to!"

He slammed the door behind him, and Chris heard him lock it from the outside. She was shaking all over by then, and she sank to the floor. But it wasn't fear that was causing her to tremble; it was anger. She had been so close! And now she wouldn't be able to help the Reeds after all. Susan and Alan would be coming by soon, but they would never manage to get her out of there.

Oh, she would get out sooner or later, she knew. All in one piece, too.

But not until it was too late.

Fourteen

"What time is it?" Susan asked nervously for what must have been the tenth time in the past fifteen minutes. She and Alan were in the pickup, headed for the Okie-Dokie Inn, on their way to their rendezvous with Chris.

"It's one-thirty," Alan replied patiently.

He, too, had been nervously watching the clock. Ever since Susan had come to him an hour earlier and told him the whole story of the "investigation" she and Chris had undertaken, and what they had found out as a result, he had been worried.

His first inclination had been to tell his parents. But they had already left for the public land auction, intending to run some errands beforehand.

Probably to keep their minds off what they're about to do, he thought sadly. Camp Pinewood has been their life for as long as I can remember—ever since I was a little boy. What they must be going through, having no other choice but to sell it!

So Susan's report of what she and her twin had discovered was heartening. Now, if only the rest of the girls' plan went off as smoothly as she seemed to think it would!

It certainly seemed simple enough. By now Chris should have had enough time to find the evidence that was necessary to prove what the Lake Majestic Realty Company had been doing all along. Once they picked her up from behind the Okie-Dokie Inn with that evidence in hand, they could race to the auction, stop his parents from signing over their land—and expose those real estate people for the crooks they really were.

Just as long as nothing went wrong. . . .

"What time is it *now*?"

Alan looked at his watch. "It's one–thirty-one. What time were we supposed to meet Chris?"

"One-thirty, on the nose. But it doesn't matter if we're a little late. She'll be there."

Alan just wished he could be as confident about this whole thing as Susan seemed to be.

As the two of them drove into the parking lot, they were both searching for Chris. Alan pulled up behind the Okie-Dokie, puzzled.

Susan, too, was surprised. "Now, *that's* funny. This is where we've both been hiding all week, while we were 'spying' on the Lake Majestic Realty office. I was sure she'd be here. . . ."

"Maybe she's still inside. Let's park over there, out of the way, and wait. She'll show up sooner or later." He glanced at his watch once again. "I just hope it's sooner. The auction starts in twenty-five minutes."

"Don't worry," Susan assured him. "Chris will come through. She *always* does."

They waited in silence. The minutes slipped by—and no Chris. Even Susan was growing fidgety.

"How long did you say it takes to drive to Town Hall from here?"

"Oh, about twenty minutes."

Susan gulped. "It's getting late, isn't it?"

Alan just nodded.

The two of them sat in the pickup truck in silence. When it was almost one–forty-five, Susan turned to Alan and said, "Look, I'm starting to get worried. I know for sure that if Chris could be here, she'd be here. Something must have happened. Something must have gone wrong. . . ."

"I'll tell you what. I'll go inside the Lake Majestic offices and see if I can find out anything."

"No—I'd better go. They might recognize you. Besides," she added, almost as if she were talking to herself, "it's my turn."

"Huh?"

"Oh, just something I'd worked out with Chris."

She walked over to the Lake Majestic Realty Company office, trying to look as casual as she could. She didn't know what she was going to say once she got inside . . . but it turned out not to matter. The door was locked.

"Hello? Hello? Anyone here?" she called.

At first, she tried to keep her voice low. But as she started to get scared, her cries grew louder and louder. "Chris, are you in there? Chris? *Chris?*"

But there was no response, only the loud hum of the air conditioners of the other offices. Even when she went around to the back of the building, she had no luck. And the window of Tom's office was closed up tight.

"She's not there, Alan," Susan reported once she got back to the truck. Her growing panic was reflected in her voice. "The whole place is deserted. I don't know *where* she could be!"

"Maybe she went on without us. Yes, that must be it. She must have gotten a ride somehow and decided not to wait for us."

"I suppose that's possible. . . . But it still doesn't sound like Chris." Susan remained baffled. And she was growing more and more worried about her sister.

"Well, at this point I guess there's nothing else for us to do but assume that she managed to get to Town Hall on her own steam. You know, your twin is one tough lady. I'm sure she's got everything under control."

"I suppose so . . . but let's go on to Town Hall anyway." She thought for a minute. "I can't explain it, but I just have a feeling that we should show up there."

"What do you mean, 'a feeling'?"

"Oh, it's just sort of a sixth sense that Chris and I have. About each other, I mean. I think it comes from our being twins."

"Sounds kind of spooky, if you ask me."

"Trust me. Let's just get over to Town Hall as fast as we can."

With a shrug, Alan started up the truck.

Twenty minutes later, they pulled into a crowded

parking lot. Apparently there were a lot of people who were interested in buying local land. Susan thought she recognized Tom's car—but she couldn't be certain. Even so, she had no doubt that he would be here. Her heart was pounding as she hurried inside with Alan in tow.

Inside, a large community room was buzzing with people. They were late, she could see; the auction was already under way. Susan scanned the crowd, looking for her twin. But she was nowhere to be seen. Her heart sank.

If Chris wasn't here and she wasn't back at the Lake Majestic offices, then where on earth *was* she? She was really getting worried now.

"There are my folks," Alan pointed out, his voice a loud whisper.

Sure enough, Jake and Olive Reed were at the front of the room, moving toward a desk on which rested a pile of official-looking papers. They both looked grim. Behind them, their faces reflecting triumph, were the three real estate agents.

"Oh, no! I think we're too late!" Susan groaned. "It looks like the deal has already been made. Your parents are about to sign over Camp Pinewood to those . . . those *criminals*!"

"Maybe we can still warn them. . . ." But Alan sounded anything but optimistic.

"Well, we might as well go over and try."

But as Susan and Alan made their way up to the front of the room, a peculiar thing happened. Tom, the real estate agent, happened to glance over and see them. All of a sudden, a look of horror crossed his face.

"It's *her*!" he cried, gripping the side of the desk

for support. He dropped the pen he had been holding in midair as he was about to sign the papers that would make Camp Pinewood his. "How did you get out?"

And then he realized something else: that this girl in the sundress walking toward him, the girl who had somehow managed to escape from that locked storeroom, had in her possession papers that could make him and his real estate company look bad. *Very* bad.

He suddenly turned beet red.

"Well, now, maybe we're being a bit too hasty here after all," he sputtered.

His two associates, Pete and Doris, looked at him in amazement.

"What are you talking about, Tom?" asked Pete, sounding annoyed. "You know we've been planning this for months. For years!"

The lawyer who was overseeing the transaction looked over at the two men, surprised. "Months? Years?" he asked, blinking with astonishment. "But this land was only put up for auction last week!"

But the others ignored him. They were too busy looking at Tom, who was growing more and more agitated.

"No," he said, "on second thought, I think we need some more time before we decide to make a big purchase like that Camp Pinewood land. In fact, I'd like to call a conference with my business associates right now, if you don't mind. . . ."

He dragged Pete and Doris away, both of them wearing expressions of amazement.

"What was that all about?" asked the lawyer.

Susan suddenly burst out laughing. She had just realized what had happened . . . and the fact that it was the very last thing she would have expected in a million years made the whole thing seem even funnier.

"Let's just say that they seemed to think I was someone else. A natural mistake, of course, but something that it never even occurred to me might happen. . . .

"Anyway, it's all for the best. Mr. and Mrs. Reed, we happen to know for a fact that those real estate agents are the people responsible for all those 'mysterious' things that have been going on at Camp Pinewood over the past few summers. They've been trying to make you lose business so you'd sell them your land—cheap. The whole thing is terribly dishonest."

"That's quite an accusation to make," the lawyer interjected with a frown. "Especially since these people happen to be some of our town's most upstanding citizens."

"Hah!" snorted Alan. "Is that why they scurried away like that just now? No, they were afraid of being exposed in public. Right here, in front of all these people." With a sweep of his arm, he indicated the roomful of local citizens who were seated in the community room, waiting for the next parcel of land to be put up for auction.

"And we have proof, too," Susan said bravely. "At least I *think* we do. First of all, we have to find my sister, Chris."

"Chris?" asked Mrs. Reed. "What does *she* have to do with all this?"

"It's a long story, but one that I hope you'll give me a chance to tell."

"I'm looking forward to it," said the lawyer. "In the meantime," he added, turning to the Reeds and handing them some papers, "why don't you hold on to the deeds to your land? As of right now, you two are still the owners."

Susan and Alan exchanged looks of relief—and triumph.

"I'll tell you what, Susan," said Alan. "How about if you stay here and tell my folks and this lawyer all about everything you two found out about the Lake Majestic Realty Company? In the meantime, I'll take the truck and try to find Chris."

"All right. But where are you going to look?"

"Back at the real estate offices. I have a feeling that this plot to 'steal' Camp Pinewood from my parents isn't the only thing those people are capable of. Maybe she's still in there, locked up or something. Didn't that man Tom say something like, 'How did she manage to get out?' At any rate, I'll tell you one thing: I wouldn't put anything past them! I'm going back over there to see what I can find out."

"Thanks." Susan squeezed his arm gratefully. "I'm sure she's all right . . . but I'll feel a lot better once she's back at camp!"

"And now," she went on, turning back to the lawyer and the Reeds, all of whom seemed anxious to hear what she had to say, "let me tell you what's been going on. I'll start at the very beginning."

Fifteen

Camp Pinewood's annual Parents' Day was held a few days after the land auction. The day dawned sunny and cool—the perfect kind of day for showing the campers' parents around, letting them get a closer look at the place where their children were making new friends and learning new things and simply having fun. Everyone had been preparing for days, and it promised to be a joyous festival.

Late that morning, the Reeds took a moment out to sit down at their kitchen table and to share a pitcher of lemonade with their son—and the camp's two most celebrated counselors, Chris and Susan Pratt.

"You know, this is easily the best Parents' Day we've ever had," said Olive Reed, putting her arms around the shoulders of both Chris and Susan. There were tears in her eyes as she spoke. "And it's all because of you two girls."

"That's right," Jake Reed agreed in a hearty voice. "If it weren't for you twins, this would be our last Parents' Day ever. *And* the last year that Camp Pinewood ever existed!"

"Well," said Susan sheepishly, "we were glad we could help. . . ."

" 'Help'! You saved Camp Pinewood!" Alan was no less grateful to the twins than his parents. "You decided that you were going to get to the bottom of all the things that had been going on here for years, and, by golly, you went ahead and did it!"

"Aw, shucks." Chris grinned. "It was easy."

"Easy!" exclaimed Olive Reed. "I don't exactly call being locked up in a storage closet for over an hour 'easy'!"

"Well . . . I suppose so," Chris said modestly. "But Tom let me out just as soon as he got back to the office, right after his hasty departure from the Public Land Auction." She chuckled to herself. "Boy, you should have seen the look on his face when he opened the door and saw that I was still in there! I thought his eyes were going to pop out of his head! He said, 'I don't believe it! There are *two* of you!' "

Chris shook her head as she remembered, her brown eyes shining with merriment. "See that? It really does pay to be a twin. Even when Sooz and I haven't actually *planned* to take advantage of the fact that we each have a double!"

"That sure was lucky." Jake Reed nodded. "If Tom hadn't mistaken Susan for Chris right before we signed those papers . . . well, I shudder to think."

"And it's lucky that Chris had the foresight to

hang on to a copy of all those memos and letters that she found in their offices," Alan said admiringly.

"Hey, after all I went through to get them, I wasn't about to leave them behind! But the funny part is, Tom never even realized that I had made two copies of each document and kept one for myself, hidden away. When I handed the whole pile of papers back to him, he just assumed I'd given up.

"Of course," she added, laughing, "he was still in shock over the fact that I'd managed to show up at Town Hall while still remaining locked up in his office. I wonder if he's managed to figure that one out yet."

"Well, I'm sure our lawyers will explain the whole thing to him. Now that we've got that evidence, Chris, we can make sure that the Lake Majestic Realty Company never tries to pull a stunt like that again."

Olive nodded in agreement with her husband. "That's right. In fact, I doubt that the Lake Majestic Realty Company will even be in existence very much longer! Especially since everyone's beginning to suspect that this kind of thing has gone on before."

"Well, I could sit around celebrating all day, but I've got things to do." Jake Reed stood up from the kitchen table. "There are a lot of parents out there who need to be given a tour of this place. And," he added with a wink, "I'm sure they'll be wanting to meet the heroes of Camp Pinewood. You know, you two have already become legends around this place!"

"I've noticed," said Alan. "The kids actually argue over whose turn it is to sit with Chris and Susan."

"Oh, Chris did most of it," Susan said, blushing. "All I did was happen to be in the right place at the right time."

"Hey, what about your 'sixth sense'?" Alan teased. "You told me you 'had a feeling' you should show up at Town Hall. I'd say that counts for plenty!"

Just then there was a knock at the screen door.

"Hello? Anybody in there?"

"Oh, it's Richard. Come on in! Door's open!"

"Thanks, Mrs. Reed. I don't mean to break up your little party, but there are a lot of parents out there who want to meet the owners of Camp Pinewood. Apparently word has spread about everything that's been going on, and there are quite a few who'd like to shake your hand!"

"Come on, Jake. Our public awaits," said Olive Reed with a smile. "Let's go attend to our camp, and let these four kids enjoy themselves."

Richard joined Alan and the twins at the kitchen table and helped himself to some lemonade. "Ummm, this looks good. But we should all save some room for the Parents' Day banquet they're setting up. I checked out the dining hall before coming over, and they've got quite a spread laid out."

"Yes, they've been working hard at it all morning," said Alan. "And even though I've been sworn to secrecy, I'm going to tell you that my parents asked me what the celebrity twins' favorites are. They want to make sure you two know you're a key part of this celebration today."

"That was sweet of them," said Susan. "But I don't know how you'd have any idea. . . ."

"Oh, no?" Alan grinned mischievously. "Let's just say that you two are not the only ones around here who have a natural talent for spying!"

"Well, the best part of all this is that now we can all take it easy and enjoy the rest of the summer," said Chris.

"Right," her twin agreed. "Now we don't have to worry about any more mysteries or pranks or prowlers in the night."

"One thing we *do* have to worry about, though," said Richard with great seriousness, "is making sure that Chris is really Chris and Susan is really Susan. Now that we all know how easy it is for you two to switch places, how can we be sure we're talking to the right twin?"

"I hadn't thought of that." Alan looked pensive. "And you two said that you've done this switching-off business before, right?"

"Oh, on occasion." Chris looked at Susan and laughed. "But we promise not to do it anymore this summer. Right, Susan?"

"Right! But wait a minute. . . . I thought I was *Chris*!"

The twins broke into hysterical laughter at the boys' confusion.

"Hey, we'd better get down to the dining hall," Richard reminded them all. "If my nose serves me correctly, I'd say it's just about time for the big Parents' Day banquet to get under way."

"I'm famished!" Chris jumped up from the

table. "And I can't wait to see those special 'goodies' that the Reeds have arranged to serve in our honor, Sooz."

Still laughing and joking, the foursome tromped down to the dining hall, Alan and Chris arm-in-arm, Richard and Susan holding hands. It *was* a real celebration, the twins had to admit. Getting rid of the "ghosts" that had been haunting Camp Pinewood for three years, saving the camp for the Reeds, and seeing that justice was done as far as the Lake Majestic Realty Company's three real estate agents were concerned were all cause for feeling triumphant. And knowing that now they could enjoy the rest of the summer, with Alan and Richard as well as each other, made everything even better.

As they walked into the dining room, there was suddenly a loud burst of applause. Indeed, word had spread quickly, and parents, campers, and counselors were all on hand to salute them. The Reeds were there, too, standing in front of a cake large enough to serve dozens of people. And written on it in big red letters were the words "Thanks, Chris and Susan!"

"Oooh, you shouldn't have!" Susan cried as she spotted the cake. The real reason for her modesty, however, was being afraid she would start to cry. But when she glanced over at her twin and saw how glassy her eyes were, she stopped worrying. At least she wouldn't be the only one!

"That's not all," said Alan in a teasing voice. He led the girls over to another table. On it was placed the biggest bowl of strawberries they had ever seen.

"Strawberries!" they cried in unison, bursting into laughter.

"Didn't you once say something about strawberries being one of the things that make summer so special?" Alan grinned knowingly.

"Of course. Strawberries . . ."

"And lemonade . . ."

"And going barefoot . . ."

"And let's not forget the really important things," Susan said seriously.

"Like what?" Chris popped a huge red strawberry into her mouth.

"Like good friends . . . and having a good time."

"Of course," said Chris. "And I can think of one more thing, too."

"What's that?"

"Having a twin sister!"

With that, the two girls leaned forward and gave each other a big, long hug.

ABOUT THE AUTHOR

Cynthia Blair grew up on Long Island, earned her B.A. from Bryn Mawr College in Pennsylvania, and went on to get a M.S. in marketing from M.I.T. She worked as a marketing manager for food companies but now has abandoned the corporate life in order to write.

She lives on Long Island with her husband, Richard Smith, and their son Jesse.